Praise for *Countdown*

"A slab of rare pulp, served nice and bloody. *Countdown* reads like an homage to Elmore Leonard from one of the hottest new voices on the crime fiction scene."

—Anthony Neil Smith, author of
Yellow Medicine and *All the Young Warriors*

Praise for the Books by Matt Phillips

"Matt Phillips speaks fluently the language of the dispossessed... His whiskey-soaked prose can at times be as slick as a man slinging snake-oil, and other times as brutal as a baseball bat to the head."

—Eryk Pruitt, author of
Hashtag and *Dirtbags*

"Phillips' writing is so multi-layered and deep... An author to watch out for."

—Regular Guy Reading Noir

COUNTDOWN

Other Titles by Matt Phillips

The Bad Kind of Lucky
Know Me from Smoke
Accidental Outlaws
Three Kinds of Fool
Redbone
Bad Luck City

MATT PHILLIPS

COUNTDOWN

All Due Respect
An imprint of Down & Out Books
3959 Van Dyke Road, Suite 265
Lutz, FL 33558
DownAndOutBooks.com

The characters and events in this book are fictitious. Any similarity to real persons, living or dead, is coincidental and not intended by the author.

Cover design by JT Lindroos

ISBN: 1-948235-84-6
ISBN-13: 978-1-948235-84-6

"...Marijuana is still illegal on the federal level. It's listed by the U.S. Drug Enforcement Administration as a 'Schedule I' drug—the same classification as LSD, ecstasy and heroin. While the federal government allows banks to work with cannabis businesses in states that have passed laws approving recreational marijuana, banks still have to file suspicious activities reports in addition to following standard banking guidelines. That means extra costs. And since the federal prohibition against marijuana is still in effect, banks fear they could be held criminally liable should a marijuana business run afoul of the law. As a result, many cannabis businesses become all-cash enterprises, with stories abounding of business people hauling duffel bags filled with cash, making them targets for robberies..."

—*The San Diego Union-Tribune*, July 5, 2017

"We're making money, okay? Making the money isn't a problem. It's more like—"

"Where to put it all."

"That's right. Where to put it all. Because the banks, they got federal insurance. And they don't touch this marijuana money. Puts them in an awkward position, if they do."

"Like, maybe the feds decide to go and do something about this marijuana thing. And if they do, shit, you get all your assets frozen. Banks get got, and so do you."

"But it's a lot of money. Like, bags of the stuff. I can't spend it too fast—I do, and the next thing I know, I got the tax man up my ass about how I'm living."

"All this money...You need to hide it."

"But where? And how?"

—Overheard in a bar

THE FOUR

ONE

Donnie Zeus Echo ordered a double cheeseburger and a lemonade, sat on the boardwalk looking at the waist-high surf and girls walking by in bikini tops and cutoff jean shorts. The way the girls wore shorts now, with the bottoms of their asses hanging out and jiggling, not too classy a look. But Echo liked to watch those asses hang and bounce down the boardwalk. Makes a decent show when you're chewing a burger and sipping something sweet, feeling that sea breeze on your face.

He wanted a cold beer but he didn't know a hamburger stand where they sold any. He'd have to go next door to the Surf Shack Tap House for that. No problem. He'd finish the burger and head over there, get a little drunk before he met with Glanson, his old battle buddy.

Glanson? Shit. Still the same fuck up who shot himself in the foot with a Russian pistol.

Echo used to be a grunt. Did a couple extended vacations in Eye-Rack. Learned to embrace the suck. Also learned to pull teeth and rip off fingernails. Arabic didn't come easy to him so Echo had to find other ways. That's another thing he learned: There's lots of ways to get a thing done.

A man has to be creative. Six years in the service and

Echo got himself an honorable discharge and not a damn thing besides. Also of note: A panther tattoo on his chest and an M16 on each wrist. Talk about a gun show. Echo drove a '99 Honda Civic with a leaky head gasket. He lived in a studio apartment off Garnet—fell asleep to the sound of coeds vomiting in the gutters. Close to the beach though. That was something he liked. And those asses hanging out. He liked those.

He chewed faster and watched a brunette waddle past him. Man, he'd like a piece of that. Something juicy besides a cheeseburger. She ignored Echo's big probing eyes, one of them a bit off point—his somewhat lazy eye. He was used to women ignoring him. Best way to get a girl's attention was to wave some money in her face. Didn't have to be much either. Enough for a decent meal and a cab ride. Simple pleasures, you know?

That's what he and Glanson should do, run down to Tijuana and get themselves a couple whores. Make the girls wear towels over their heads so the two grunts could pretend they were back in Eye-Rack. Good times, baby. The bad thing about Middle Eastern girls is they hold still while you fuck them. Far as he knew, Mexican girls bucked like wild horses.

Yes, sir—he craved some señoritas with some decent ta-tas.

Echo finished his burger, sucked down lemonade until the straw whistled. He watched a skinny blonde roll past on some roller blades. Not bad. But it'd be better with a few beers in him.

He stood to go next door, careful to cover the bulge of the .45 tucked into his waistband. He touched the gun tenderly through the fabric of his Hawaiian shirt—oh, you wanna wanna lay her?—and smiled. Echo knew Glanson.

Sure he did. But that didn't mean he trusted Glanson.

No fucking way. Not in this life. And not in the next one.

TWO

Abbicus Glanson had a small dick and he knew it. Sure, it bothered him. The way to make up for that—in Glanson's mind—was to act crazy as shit, draw as much attention as you can. That worked in a war zone. It worked damn well. Not so much back home—in *Murica*, as Glanson liked to call it. Not when he needed a job, money, a place of residence.

When he left the service, Glanson had a neon green Honda CBR crotch rocket, three shotguns, and a respectable collection of pocket knives.

He rode the bike cross-country, decided to rent an apartment in San Diego. He liked the weather and, growing up in the Midwest, he dreamed about living near the Pacific Ocean. Didn't use it much, but he liked to know all his childhood buddies back home were talking shit about him living in California. Let those suckers freeze their asses off in April. Glanson wore flip-flops and board shorts every fucking day, walked around in December with his shirt off.

Fuck Glanson? No—fuck the small-town Midwest.

Fuck you, motherfuckers.

Still, Glanson had a bitch of a time finding steady work. He could always go back to the war zone with a private firm, but you can't wear flip-flops and fuck surfer girls in Eye-Rack. About the best you can do is smoke a joint and drink a forty oz. But you had to avoid being killed.

That was the big thing, the hard part.

So, no private security gig in Eye-Rack. No steady job. Nothing. Nada.

But then he met a guy at Ray's in Ocean Beach, a favorite locals spot for live music. Glanson liked Ray's for the drink specials and the scent of marijuana hanging in the air.

This short bald guy, burly as hell in a blue tank, nods at Glanson and says, "Where you do yours, amigo?"

"My what?"

The guy points at a tattoo on Glanson's wrist: An M16 wrapped by a hissing serpent. "Your tat, man. Where'd you get it?"

"Eye-Rack," Glanson says. "What's it to you?"

The guy turns around and lifts his tank over his head. His back is covered with a detailed soldier in full body armor. The soldier's eyes squint at Glanson and the gun in his hand is pointed right at Glanson's heart.

Glanson says, "Holy shit."

The guy lowers his shirt and turns around, says, "Fucking A. Grunt through and through, baby."

Glanson got lucky. Turns out this other grunt—Abel Sendich—hit on an innovative business idea. With the legalization of marijuana in California, and the federal illegality of the drug, there's a teeny weeny money problem. You can grow weed. You can sell it. You can smoke it and you can eat it. You can do just about whatever you want with it. But the money you make off it— there's the motherfucking rub. You can't put it in a bank because the IRS will start asking important questions. You can't keep it at the dispensary—that's asking for an ass whipping.

So, what do you do with it?

"Fuck if I know," Glanson says. "You gotta launder it some way, clean it."

"Whatever you do," Abel says deep into his fifth beer, "You got to move it, and you got to store it. No two ways about that—move the money, store the money."

Okay, then. Glanson thought about that for about half a beer. Next thing he knows, Abel's asking Glanson if he needs a job. Bada-fucking-bing.

Yes. He. Does.

Two weeks later, Glanson found himself wearing a 9mm and a collared black Dickies shirt, watching the parking lot outside Acee's Apothecary on Thirty-Second and Adams. "Might as well do it now," he said. "Light traffic and it's the end of business."

Next to him, in the driver's seat of the white Econoline van, Abel nodded. "I'll pull in along the door. Make sure you unclip the nine. Be ready, Glanson. We haven't got pinged yet, but a couple guys got shitcanned up in North County just last week."

"I read about that," Glanson said. Two private security guys shot down by 'bangers knocking over a dispensary in Del Mar, of all fucking places. The 'bangers escaped. The security guys were still sleeping. Taking permanent naps. "Came at them with automatics."

Abel chuckled. "We need to gear up, baby. I'm looking to get us some more shotties."

"Need a fucking grenade one of these days," Glanson said.

Abel didn't say shit to that. He fired up the van, let it

roll away from the curb, drift left across the street, and bounce into the parking lot. He stopped. "Your chariot awaits."

Glanson unclipped the holster for his nine, rested his right hand on the gun.

He opened the passenger door and walked briskly toward the steel-reinforced door, pushed it open and disappeared into Acee's Apothecary.

This new job Glanson had—it paid the bills and it came with a perk: Mary Jane in spades.

THREE

Jessie Jessup didn't come from money. She came from three generations of cattle ranchers in east Texas. She was a woman, but for all her beauty—petite at five-three and a hundred seven pounds—Jessie came from men. She was of men—hard fucking men. At thirty-seven years old, she still carried a hint of her Texas drawl, but a decade living in SoCal had drained most of that lilt from her speech.

Jessie's daddy taught her to invest in herself, in her own operation. He used to say you don't got a damn thing until you can't help but give yourself all the money you make. That didn't make much sense to Jessie when she waited tables, or when she sold used cars, or when she worked at a place called Gino's Nursery.

It made sense now, after an ex-lover named Amos French taught Jessie a growing technique called aquaponics. That is to say, French taught Jessie how to grow weed using fish—that's right, fucking fish. And you could do it inside, away from the prying eyes of neighbors and cops.

Turned out, Jessie had herself a green thumb. Two green thumbs.

She grew that dank motherfucking weed.

But Jessie didn't have any street smarts. Hell, she knew how to tell a horny cowpoke to fuck off, and she knew how to save a horse and ride a cowboy when she needed to, but she didn't know how to negotiate the gangs and woe-be-gones of the gritty SoCal underbelly.

That's what LaDon was for. LaDon was big, he was black, and he was mean as shit when it came down to it. He also knew where they could open a dispensary operation and keep it under wraps. No way Jessie could get a legit dispensary license. That shit was too complicated. She took one look at the paperwork after reading through Proposition 64 and decided she'd do this shit on the sly.

Enter LaDon, another regular at The Zip Zap Bar in City Heights. He used to tease her about drinking cosmos in a dive bar, but they got along. Sure, LaDon wanted a piece of her, but he also had an ex-wife and daughter.

Jessie liked to fuck and run. She was a one-night stand kind of girl. That made LaDon off-limits.

So, here the two of them were, waiting around after seven o'clock—quitting time, dammit—for the war vets to show up and get the cash. She watched LaDon sip a Diet Coke and pick at his fingernails. He had a Taser in his top drawer and fists big enough to crush a pumpkin. Their operation was bare bones, but at any one time, they were sitting on twenty K or more in straight cash. That's decent bait for a stick-up boy, especially in the neighborhood LaDon chose for their place of business. The dispensary was off University Avenue, a small office next to a tire shop and below two studio apartments. All day, Jessie cringed at the little kids stomping on the ceiling. Since they opened this spot two months ago and started working social media and Weed Maps, they'd cleared nearly sixty K in sales.

And shit was ramping up.

Jessie shut off her computer, leaned back in her office chair, and said, "LaDon, you ever think about going on a diet?"

He twirled the Diet Coke can so she could read the label: "The fuck you think this is, woman?"

"That's diabetes waiting to happen is what that is."

"I already have the diabetes, sister. It runs in the family."

"Only thing that runs in your family is a sweet tooth."

LaDon stared at her with menace eyes. "You going to cook me dinner this week?"

"Wednesday, baby," Jessie said. "I got some vegan pasta and a couple of—"

"What's that now?" LaDon shifted in his seat. The floor creaked with his weight. He planted his elbows on the steel desk, closed one eye in confusion.

"Vegan pasta." Jessie watched him, a smile barely visible at the corners of her mouth.

"Uh-uh, Jess. I want some motherfucking ribs. Or that thing you made last time..." He snapped his fingers searching for the name.

"Marsala," she said. "Chicken marsala."

"That was some good white people food. I'll eat that whenever. But vegan pasta? Oh, hell no."

Jessie laughed, blew a lock of brown hair from her eyes. "You might like it, big boy."

LaDon shook his head, checked his cell for the time. "Where these motherfuckers at?"

"Making the Friday rounds," Jessie said.

"Let me get this straight," LaDon said, "These dudes are keeping our money with a lot of other drug dealers' money? And you're good with that?"

"They're a security start up. They're solving an important problem."

"Sixty K ain't never gonna be a problem for me, Jess."

Jessie shrugged. They couldn't keep the money in the office—in fact, it was LaDon who told her that. But he didn't like the guy who came to see her about holding their money. Bald guy named Abel. He was a fast talker and sarcastic as hell. But it wasn't him who sold Jessie on the service.

It was Abel's partner, a tall eucalyptus-looking guy—white-ish skin and thin, wispy hair—named Glanson. Another war vet. She guessed they served together.

Jessie liked Glanson. He was good looking and had honest eyes. She hoped he was coming to get their pick up this evening.

It'd be nice to see Glanson.

LaDon said, "I think it's because you like the tall one."

Jessie rolled her eyes. She turned around in the office chair and began to unlock the safe. "You know I'm the kind of girl who does it one night at a time—I'm not looking for a ball and chain."

"Whatever you say." LaDon leaned back in his seat and closed his eyes.

Jessie finished punching in the combination and the safe door creaked open to reveal six stacks of money bound by thick rubber bands. She reached inside and began to pull the money out, tossing stack after stack into a gray duffel bag.

LaDon took a toothpick from a tray on his desk, began to run it along his hairline. "We gonna do six figures this month?"

"Not this month," Jessie said. "But business is fucking booming. We're looking at twenty K."

"And you need any help with the grow?"

"I could use someone to do my laundry, clean up the apartment for me."

"Fuck that," LaDon said. "I'm busy."

Jessie finished with the money, zipped the bag closed, and secured it with a small combination lock. She turned and looked at LaDon. "I've been wondering...you got a nickname, LaDon?"

LaDon smiled that nice big smile of his. "They call me Captain Groove," he said. "You wanna know why?" He shimmied in his seat.

Jessie laughed, she couldn't help it. "You smart ass..."

FOUR

LaDon Marcus Garvey Charles, Black & Mild glowing red between his lips, pulled his gold Cutlass into the parking lot outside The Zip Zap Bar. He backed into a corner spot and sat listening to James Brown for a cool hard minute. A maroon Dodge Neon pulled into the lot and parked beside him. LaDon watched the driver, a black guy with dreads, take one last nip on a roach and leave the car unlocked as he walked into the bar. Another productive citizen on the prowl, LaDon said to himself. Shit, another potential customer for the dispensary. He'd toss a business card—their address and a cryptic message: *For all your botanical necessities*—on the guy's front seat. Most times, LaDon left the card on the windshield, but why not show how trustworthy he was by leaving this one in the car?

Like saying, don't you worry, homeboy—I ain't out to get you.

LaDon shut off the Cutlass, sat listening to the non-silence of the city. Like a buzz that won't go away, a fucking mechanical bee buzz. LaDon grew up in south-east San Diego and he was getting to the point he wanted out of the city. He did the black thing, whatever that was: Played weak side linebacker on a city champ high school team, did his two years at City College, and worked private security since. That is, until he ran into the white girl—Jessie Jessup with the sweet white-girl rump. LaDon never in his life did jail time and he never did wrong. At least, not to anybody who didn't do him wrong first. A few years back he encountered some issues with a clique of Crips down in Chula, but that got resolved. Nothing a shottie and a semi-auto couldn't correct. And LaDon came correct, that was for damn sure.

He still had the shotgun—a pump-action Savage—stashed in the Cutlass's trunk. The pistol he dumped on a fishing run out to the kelp beds. That story wasn't something LaDon thought too much about; it was a thing that happened to him and he made it out with his life.

It's a win if you're still breathing.

LaDon felt good about what he was doing now, helping Jessie run the dispensary. Funny to call it that, some official-sounding name. What it was, and LaDon didn't kid himself about this, was a drug spot. He and Jessie (mostly Jessie) were running a drug corner, and LaDon played Mr. Muscle. He didn't believe weed was a drug. Not like the way heroin was a drug, the way crack was a drug. LaDon had cousins in prison, a brother dead in the ground, and he knew what drugs did to lives. See, weed came from the ground—you didn't need to process it or change it with chemicals. It didn't come from a fucking lab neither. All natural up in this motherfucker. And, to LaDon, that seemed alright. It seemed better than all the other shit. What LaDon and Jessie did was organic, free-trade, non-GMO, gluten-fucking-free. Take that and smoke it, baby.

But LaDon was smart. He convinced Jessie the money

they would make—all that cash they needed to store and eventually wash for legitimacy—needed protection. And LaDon thought: That's all me, right? Wrong. Jessie took his suggestion as something else, and she had these two war vets on the payroll now. The one guy, the bald one with a lippy tone, made LaDon nervous. He walked around like all the 'bangers LaDon ever knew, a scowl on his face and darting eyes, a man looking for his next fight. The tall vet, man who looked like a sapling, LaDon didn't mind. He was alright except that Jessie had the hots for him. LaDon kept thinking he was going to get some of that sweet white ass from Jessie, but now he knew better. LaDon wasn't Jessie's type.

It's all good. LaDon could take it.

LaDon had a lady he stayed with in Lemon Grove. He also had a little girl named Sonia and an ex-wife worked out at the county jail. He got to see Sonia on the weekends, every other that is. The other two weekends a month LaDon went fly or saltwater fishing. A thing he got into in his mid-twenties. Decided he wanted to catch a fish one day, found himself on a party boat roping calico bass off the coast. That was LaDon's sole addiction—fishing. Everything else was a means to that end, including these few drinks he was about to put under the hood.

LaDon took his regular seat at The Zip Zap Bar—corner beneath the old TV—and ordered a bourbon and Coke without ice. He watched Zim mix the drink and eyeball a twenty-something lady hovering over the pinball machine. She wore a red spaghetti-strap blouse and tight jeans, moved her hips like a metronome.

LaDon scooped up the drink when Zim set it on the bar and said, "You know the lady playing games over there?" LaDon's big smile crept across his face.

Zim said, "What, you going to try for an interception?"

"Don't pretend you made any progress on the thing, Zim. Plus, you got to work all night."

"I work until midnight, motherfucker."

LaDon sipped his drink. "It's a wrap long before midnight."

"Man, whatever," Zim said. "Jessie coming by tonight, or what?"

"Said she'd come by. We just wrapped up work. She's got a thing for a guy who does some stuff for us. When I left, she was waiting to get all goochie-goo with him. You know how that is."

"A business like that..." Zim trailed off and watched a couple walk in, park themselves in a booth along the back wall. The man wore tight reflective pants and the woman looked confused. Her hair was mussed and her eyes were dark with fatigue. Zim nodded at Cera, a young cocktail waitress studying her cell phone at the end of the bar. Cera rolled her eyes and stomped toward the couple. "A business like that," Zim continued, "you got to be careful who you let in, right?"

"That's what it is," LaDon said finishing his drink. He planted the glass in the palm of his left hand, swept the moisture from it, and wiped his forehead. "Lots of things you watch when you're doing the Lord's work."

Zim made a sound on one side of his mouth. "Only God I know is the almighty dollar. Makes me think, too, you got the ten Gs we talked about? I'm going to start us out small, wash that little by little. You and Jessie get it back clean in a month. Pressed with starch, brother."

"A whole month to wash ten Gs?" LaDon said. "You doing every dollar by hand?"

Zim waved a hand at the near-empty bar, settled his eyes on Cera, trying to get a drink order from the couple in the booth. "You know I ain't do much volume, LaDon."

LaDon turned around to study the place. The man in reflective pants was lounging against the seat, his head tilted toward one shoulder. The woman rearranged a stack of cocktail napkins. Cera tapped one foot and chomped bubble gum. The man with dreads and the Dodge Neon sat a few stools down from LaDon, his hair dangling in his face as he stared into his beer bottle. The lady at the pinball machine swung her hips back and forth as she played. LaDon said, "It's like she's riding a horse."

"What's that?"

LaDon lifted his chin at the woman.

"Might be she wants to ride a horse," Zim said.

LaDon nodded. "Giddy-the-fuck up, huh? Look, you mind making me two bourbon and Cokes? Give me one with ice, alright?"

"For the lady?"

"That's right," LaDon said. "For my new lady."

FIVE

Echo was three beers deep when he saw Glanson enter the Surf Shack Tap House and swivel his head looking for his old battle buddy. Glanson was still in decent shape, those shoulders hunched up beneath a thin collared shirt. The shirt, like Echo's own, hung out of the man's pants. If he knew Glanson, he had a pistol wedged right up against his small-ass dick. Glanson was actual bat shit crazy. Like, live in a fucking straitjacket kind of crazy.

Echo remembered Glanson using his rifle to punch a house full of holes in Eye-Rack. And he kept punching those holes when he heard the screams. Not just men, either.

He might be crazy, but Glanson knew how to act sane.

Yeah, Echo thought, the man knows how to act sane. As fuck.

Echo stood and walked toward the restaurant's waiting area where Glanson was querying a teenage hostess. Echo tried to shake off the war memory, all those high-pitched screams and wails. He tried to think about the double-double from earlier and the .45 pushing warm and heavy against the small of his back. After a few seconds, he caught Glanson's crazy-sane gaze and said, "What up, buddy?"

* * *

"It's entrepreneurship is what it is," Glanson said. He played with his collar for a moment, brought a shaking hand down to his beer bottle, lifted it to his big mouth. He sipped and licked his lips. "Plain old American innovation, you want to know the truth. I mean, I'm not saying I'm getting rich off the fucking business. It's hourly, you know. But it's..." He paused, sniffed hard through one nostril. "It's a job, man. It's a purpose, okay?"

Echo watched Glanson fidget in his seat. He seemed jumpy, nervous. That in itself didn't surprise him, but the way Glanson kept looking at the restaurant's entrance did.

Echo finished his beer, snapped his fingers at a cute brunette waitress with her floral print skirt riding high on her ass. She wasn't bad—he planned to tip decent and leave her his cell number. The brunette smirked at him and nodded. She'd bring him another beer, but God was he annoying. Echo meant to be like that. Women can't resist the biggest asshole in the room.

"You called a meeting with me so I could compliment your fucking résumé?" Echo stared bayonets at Glanson. "Why the fuck are we here? A couple beers between buddies?"

"Isn't that enough, Ec?" Glanson's knee bounced so hard the cocktail table shook.

"What the fuck is wrong with you?"

Glanson played stupid. "What are you saying?"

Echo said, "Tell you what I remember about the war: I remember dry heaving in the mornings, searching dead bodies for extra ammo. I remember the sound of IEDs, man. I remember kids screaming. Women, too. And what I'm wondering is—"

"You didn't need to say that."

"What I'm wondering," Echo continued, "is why the dumb fuck sitting across from me is trying to bring all this shit back up in my head. I'm wondering—"

"That's not what I called you for, man."

"I'm wondering why we're drinking beers and trying hard not to kill each other."

Glanson shook his head.

The waitress set a beer in front of Echo without saying anything. Echo said, "That's perfect, sweetie." He watched her slide into the sea of guests.

Glanson said, "I'm telling you about the job, Ec."

"The job. Yeah, that's fine. Question is, why the fuck are you telling me about the job?"

Glanson looked at the restaurant entrance once more, turned back to his battle buddy. He bit his bottom lip, drained his beer. He left the bottle on the table and crossed his arms tight across his chest. "I said, I'm not getting rich. It's a job is all it is. And, well, shit. It's a job, Ec, but you wouldn't believe the fucking money we pick up and hold for these fuckers. I'm talking, like, six figures, okay? And that's daily. We got a storage unit down in National City with stacks of fucking cash—I'm going to say a few million. You look at the money, and you count it up in your head, okay? You're imagining this shit, and you can't count as high as you can imagine. It's that kind of mind-fuck."

"I'll believe that when I see it."

Glanson uncrossed his arms, dug into his pants pockets. He set his cell phone on the table and brought up an image. He turned the phone so Echo could see the screen. "There you go, Ec. Believe what you see, man."

Echo leaned over the table. The image, taken from about hip height, showed a dark space with a roll-top door halfway closed. In the shadows, a man leaned down over a stack of black duffel bags. He had a clipboard and pencil in his hands. Echo slid the cell phone back to Glanson and said, "You trying to tell me all that's cash? Every single bag?"

"Every single bag."

"It's small bills, or what?"

Glanson nodded, threw his nervous gaze around the restaurant.

"What do they do with the money?"

Glanson shrugged. "You can't put it in the bank. IRS starts asking questions and it's bad juju. They got to find a way to put it back in through legit means."

"You hold it until they find a way to…"

"Wash it, basically. I mean, it's small bills. But it has to be laundered back into circulation through a legitimate business."

Echo needed to think. Okay, so what did Glanson want from him? A partner, maybe? Did they need more muscle? Fuck an hourly wage. He could go back overseas and guard contractors for good money. Sure, he needed to dodge bullets and watch fuckers pray to Allah, but it was still money. Any plan that included him and Glanson together only made sense for get-out money. Money that got him out—and for fucking good.

"And this money just waits for us to pick it up, Ec. I'm telling you: It's too fucking easy."

Echo gulped half his new beer. "Who's the guy in the picture?"

"That's my boss. Abel started the business, brought me in. Pays jackshit…"

"Tell me what it is then: You want to rob your fucking boss? You don't think he'll—"

"Not him, Ec." For the first time, Glanson's eyes bored into Echo. They were deep brown eyes with unsteady irises. His cheeks hardened beside his nose and a long vertical wrinkle deepened on his forehead. "No way I'd rob my boss. What I want to do is start a stick-up business. I want to rob the dispensaries."

Echo sat in deep thought for a long time. He watched the people around him lift drinks to their mouths, smile and laugh at each other. He saw the brunette waitress roll her eyes at an old man in a golf shirt. Before, the brunette made Echo hard. He wanted her. Now, it was the money that made him hard. He wanted it. He imagined how heavy it would be across his shoulders as he boarded a boat down to Mexico. He saw himself in a cheap motel room, a bottle of tequila on the bedside table, counting wrinkled twenties, tens...the occasional hundred-dollar bill.

Finally, Echo said, "You keep looking around—what for?"

Glanson smiled and, in that crazy-sane way, said: "Ghosts, man. I'm watching for them ghosts."

SIX

Jessie poured herself a glass of four-dollar sparkling wine and sipped while staring out her kitchen window. The street was jammed with cars parallel parked and bratty kids riding bicycles and skateboards up and down the block, everybody shouting. Jessie lived in a second floor walk up, paid fourteen hundred every month to hear endless sirens, husbands shouting at wives, and the police and news choppers buzzing like giant insects through the evenings and early mornings.

Sometimes she wondered: The fuck am I paying for?

And thirteen years working didn't do shit for her. Until she started at the plant nursery. Jessie had a 401(k) that might last a year when she retired and a savings account for overdraft protection. Without the dispensary and the marijuana plants growing in her spare bedroom, Jessie figured she was worth the price of a used-new Toyota Camry. That's if she sold her own Toyota.

To Jessie, this whole green thumb hobby meant stability, semi-wealth, maybe even an honest-to-God retirement fund.

She finished her sparkling wine, poured another glass. The bubbles fizzed, spilled over the glass and poured onto the tile countertop. Jessie ran a finger through the liquid, brought it to her lips and slurped. Okay, Jessie, you got the pot thing swinging now, but what else do you got?

She smiled a little, liked how the alcohol touched her insides. She'd got this good-looking war vet dude, Abbicus Glanson. He came in again today and Jessie felt that upside down feeling in her chest. Like being in sixth grade again and seeing the cutest guy in the class. He comes in with that black pistol hanging against his thigh, one sloping hand gripped on it—those pasty knuckles not even white with fear. He's got this loose shirt on, but Jessie likes how it shows his muscled shoulders. And he's laid back. He comes in, looking to the left side of the office, seeing that LaDon's gone for the day.

Abbicus—no, she's going to call him Abbie—looks at her with those hard-soft green eyes and says, "I'm here for the money, sister. And whatever else you got."

And Jessie's giggling. Like that sixth-grade girl. She's blushing probably, and she's reaching around behind her desk to grab the duffel bag. She slaps it onto the desk, comes around, and leans back against her pile of money. Knows her tits are pushed up high in her blouse and her tight black pants hint at the perfect shape of her pussy. She's staring at the man and already imagining how she'd moan with him inside her. And what the fuck is this sixth-grade kind of crush going on? She's wondering about her own sanity. Get sane, Jessie.

Glanson's walking up to her, pressing against her, reaching around to grab the bags. His breath presses hard into her face—nicotine and al pastor, the sweet scent of the SoCal working man.

And...God, he feels fucking good pressing into her. She feels the shape of the gun up inside her thigh. Likes it. Gets off a little on it. And then he's walking backwards, a smile coming to his face. And she moves toward him, says, "You should come by my place tonight."

Okay. Okay.

And later, a glass of cheap sparkling wine in her hand, she felt that same burn inside her, a brief wetness emerging between her legs like sweat on her wine glass. She looked out the window again, saw the kids riding back and forth like banshees. Jessie shut the curtains, walked with her wine down the hall to peek into the spare bedroom.

When she opened the door, the aroma smacked her in the face. Ah, that perfect, dank, delicious, money-making, weed-grow smell she loved so fucking much. She licked her lips, took pleasure in counting the forty plants lined up in aquarium tanks, all the tiny fish in the water below giving nutrients to her perfect nuggets of cannabinoid deliciousness.

Jessie Jessup loved growing her some marijuana.

And she loved selling it even more. Who'd have thought an east Texas girl could start a mini-marijuana empire in her late thirties? Not me, Jessie thought, but here the fuck I am. She laughed to herself, sipped more wine and shut the door quietly, like a mother trying not to wake her children. In the bedroom, Jessie shimmied out of her tight black pants, let her pink panties fall to the floor. She tossed her blouse on the pile of clothes and unsnapped her bra, let it fall. She walked into the bathroom, stared at herself in the mirror for a long un-interrupted moment. She looked good—not perfect, but good. For her age. And Jessie felt good. She liked the way her eyes tapered into crow's feet when she laughed and how her hips jutted out from her still-somewhat-flat stomach. What she wanted—and what she hadn't had in a long fucking time—was a man. Not that she needed a man. She'd never needed a fucking thing.

Jessie always took care of herself. She waitressed, bartended, dressed hair, managed a jewelry store. Jackie-of-all-fucking trades. But Jessie also wanted a man—was that so bad?

And you know what? Fuck it if that didn't make her a feminist.

Look what feminism got Jessie: A two-bedroom apartment on the bad side of town and a temperamental Toyota with a hundred eighty-seven thousand miles on a rebuilt engine. Jessie wanted to fuck.

And Abbie better come and do what he promised.

She walked into her closet and found a green slip with thin over-the-shoulder straps. She slipped it on over her head and checked herself in the mirror again. She liked the way the green fabric rested against her thighs and showed just a hint of her small nipples—half-coins with points inside them. See what Abbie says when she answers the door in this fucking thing.

Another sip of sparkling wine. And another.

Okay, she thought, he better get here soon.

It was almost ten and he was supposed to be there already. But Jessie knew he was finishing his work day. Alright, I can wait, she thought, but I sure as shit don't have to—do I?

No.

Jessie tilted the wine glass, dipped two fingers into the bubbly liquid. She stared into her own eyes through the mirror, ran her wet fingers along the inside of one tan thigh. Okay, she thought, okay. Her fingers ran upwards— slow, so fucking slow—and stopped. She took a deep breath, pressed those two wet fingers between her legs.

Somewhere far off, Jessie heard herself moan.

SEVEN

After his few beers with Glanson, Echo walked north on the boardwalk toward the pier. He stopped in a liquor store with neon flashing messages about tequila and American-made beer, bought himself a small bottle of El Jimador. He was surprised they had it there. Most times, he found El Jimador down in Tijuana in one of the bodegas off Avenida Revolución.

He kept the bottle tucked under his arm and wandered through people on skateboards and beach cruisers, pretended not to eyeball the girls in ass-high shorts and flip-flops. The air was slightly wet from the sea, cool and refreshing in the night. Many of the shops along the boardwalk—a cement walk these days—were closed down for the night. A block east, Echo heard the rowdy bar crowd. It was a mixture of live music, lame pickup lines, and the general din of young people trying to find somebody else to fuck.

Echo reached the pier and took another sip of tequila, decided to walk out and listen to the moving black sea. The pier creaked and moaned as he sauntered past the closed souvenir and bait shops. In a snack bar restaurant about halfway down the pier, he saw a solitary line cook wiping down his kitchen behind a lighted glass window.

The man puffed a cigarette, stopped every few seconds to exhale. It was illegal to smoke in a restaurant here in California, but Echo admired the man for his fuck-it-all attitude. Long day at work and you want yourself a smoke.

Echo kept walking and thought about Glanson's idea: You want to rob dispensaries not for the product, but for the money—what's the risk? You got to worry about the security guards or Rambo-ass dispensary owners. You got to worry about witnesses, okay. But the real risk is some gung-ho pothead swinging a shottie on you and pulling the trigger. Some free love, Jah love punk bitch with too little brains to see his own hyper-capitalist personal contradictions. Free love? Sure. Long as we get paid for it. So, why the fuck not rob them? Echo couldn't think of a reason, not besides the "maybe I'll get shot" part. Fuck it—he'd been through that and survived.

He reached the end of the pier, leaned over the railing, and stared at the waves rushing beneath the pilings. A few night fisherman huddled to his right, a lone man in dark clothes to his left. Echo turned and saw the man—an Asian man with a huge fishing rod—giving him the once-over. Out here, the scent of dead fish was strong. That, and the ever-present aroma of bird shit. Echo sniffed hard, nodded at the man, and turned back to the moving black sea.

He took another pull from the bottle of El Jimador, realized it was half-empty already. That was fine—it would start Echo's night off right. He didn't sleep much. Instead, he spent a lot of time in strip clubs and dive bars, looking for ways to spend his Eye-Rack savings. Most nights he used a ride-share service. No reason to drive drunk in a big city, not even for a PTSD freak like Echo. That's what he called himself when he was drunk: The PTSD freak.

Fuck it, he thought, we all gotta be something.

A man in a trucker's cap approached and leaned on the railing a few feet from Echo. The man wore loose-fitting pants, sandals, and a long-sleeve shirt for hiking. The shirt's fabric made flapping noises in the wind. The man said, "Beautiful night, huh?"

Echo didn't respond.

"You look drunk," the man said.

Echo turned, leaned one hip against the pier railing. "What business is that of yours?"

The man shrugged. "Just looking for something to talk about. I wish I was drunk."

Echo motioned at the shoreline, looked for a second at the glowing lights. The night life din reached them here but it was more subdued, like a radio playing softly in a cheap motel room. "Plenty of places to get lit back that way." He drank from his tequila bottle.

"Or you could share," the man said.

Echo nodded thoughtfully.

"Just a little," the man said. "To wet my whistle."

Echo moved toward the man, held the bottle out for him. A breeze riffled through Echo's short hair and he saw the man turn slightly, glare out from beneath the bent brim of the trucker's hat.

Echo knew the look. He saw the serrated knife before it flipped open to grin at him. He sensed the man lunging before he did so, and Echo swung the tequila bottle hard, down and forward, until it smashed the brim of the man's hat into the fleshy bridge of his nose. He hit the man twice more—both times in the face. It was too dark to see the blood, but Echo knew it was there, dripping down through the pier's planks and splashing into the sea below them. The man groaned once and began to whimper.

Echo cleared his throat, looked up to see the small group of fisherman staring at him. In turn, each man looked back to the sea and the thin etching of his own fishing line tailing into the black water. Echo turned around and the Asian man watched him for a moment, nodded. He, too, turned back to the sea. Echo looked down once more at the whimpering man with the bleeding face.

Echo said, "In case you still want to know—I'm drunk as fuck."

He left the man there to bleed and stumbled back the way he'd come, toward the glowing lights and party noises.

He thought about bags of money. He didn't feel bad about the man bleeding at the end of the pier.

No, Echo felt pretty fucking good. Sometimes, even PTSD freaks feel pretty fucking good.

EIGHT

After meeting his old battle buddy down at the beach, Glanson fired up his crotch rocket and motored east on the eight freeway to see Jessie Jessup. He was surprised the woman had the hots for him but it was easy to see that she did. Third week in a row Glanson went to get her marijuana money and the woman is dressed in a skimpy top and pushing her hips out toward him.

He never got it offered like that. Not even after boot camp when he walked around in uniform.

But a dark sinking feeling spread in Glanson as he reached ninety miles per hour and weaved through light evening traffic. If Jessie wanted him that bad it meant—sooner or later—he needed to remove his pants. Glanson always did well with women up until that point. But when he removed his pants, most women smirked and said, "Oh." Either that or some other single syllable, anti-climactic expression. Once, Glanson even got "Huh" from a coed down in Miami Beach.

If he got past that with a lady—if she, sort of, kind of, didn't mind—Glanson was alright.

But he didn't always get past it. Or rather, the ladies didn't get past it.

Glanson thought being born was a funny thing. You

get what you get, and that's it.

Maybe he could get Jessie hot enough she wouldn't care. Maybe she'd want it so bad he could plunge into her, plow her like a thumb into a watermelon. He doubted it, but you never knew.

Glanson slowed and took an exit ramp without using his turn signal. He zipped around a slow hybrid car—fucking wackos—and made a right turn onto a surface street. At the next stoplight, he rolled up to the crosswalk between a beat-to-shit Toyota pickup truck and a red, early 2000s Mitsubishi sedan bumping Tupac. Glanson made note of the tire shops, smog check stations, and cheap corner stores. Looked like Jessie didn't live in the hip part of the city.

Glanson didn't know the city well. His new job was changing that, but he was surprised to find Jessie lived out this way, even with her dispensary operating in a shitty neighborhood. Glanson figured you take your business to the clientele, but you don't live with your customers.

The light turned green and Glanson throttled into second gear, took the next right, and found Jessie's apartment building after cruising past a series of unlighted buildings, their address numbers either missing or obscured in darkness. He parked his bike at an angle against the curb and sat there with the engine off, listening to the night.

Far off, he heard the gasoline whisper of the freeway. On top of that was the staccato hammer of the police chopper above him. Glanson looked up, saw the chopper's spotlight sweeping a grid a few blocks east. Somebody on the run, he thought. Sounds of children and cooking floated from Jessie's apartment building, and Glanson watched the windows thinking he might get a glance of her naked silhouette. What are you, he asked himself, a romantic motherfucker?

He shook his head, dismounted the bike. His helmet swung from one hand as he walked through the courtyard of dead grass and thirsty plants. One palm tree waved like a skeletal finger high above the building. He slowed and checked the apartment numbers, saw that Jessie was on the second floor. He reached the staircase and started upwards. You're no romantic motherfucker, he thought. No goddamn way. You're a stick-up man is what you are. You used to be a goddamn *Murican* hero, a fucking robo-soldier, but you got out of that with almost nothing. With barely anything. Except your life. And now you're going to rob marijuana dispensaries.

Yes-fucking-sir, you are.

Fuck romance…Fuck romance…Fuck romance…

The phrase ran through Glanson's head as he reached the top of the staircase, saw Jessie's apartment number, 2A, on the nearest door. He walked up to it, saw the white button for the buzzer. Thought: A real man bangs on a fucking door. And if he needs to, he bangs it off the hinges. How'd that be? Kick down the door, rush in, and rip her panties to shreds.

Fuck her silly right there on the shaggy carpet.

The size of his dick wouldn't matter then, would it?

Fuck romance…

Glanson pounded the door three times with his fist. Above him, the chopper sound faded, stretched elsewhere into the night. He heard the deadbolt click, saw the door handle turn. And when Jessie opened the door in a clingy green slip, Glanson said, "I bet you a dozen red roses me and you are meant for each other. What do you say, Jessie? Want to take that bet?"

NINE

LaDon found himself putting his big hands on the lady's cherry-drop ass, slid them up to the small of her back, down again onto that ripe booty fruit. He felt her breath on the front of his neck, the lady swaying to Otis Redding on The Zip Zap Bar's sound system. LaDon swirled her toward the back of the bar, where the shadows fell over a booth—the only light a green glow from a neon Rolling Rock sign. He said, "Ginny: Where the hell have you been all my life? I swear I've known you since birth."

Ginny—in her early twenties now that LaDon had a long look at her—laughed a bit from half-down her throat. She was tipsy, and maybe getting drunk. "Augusta, Georgia," she said. "Sitting around and slapping away mosquitoes."

"And now you're out here in the city." LaDon sat her down in the booth, slid in opposite her. He watched her eyelids fall slowly, lift to reveal pearl eyes in the green light. She rested her head on an elbow. LaDon smiled at her—that big bright smile he knew white people wanted from him. "What brings you over into my neighborhood, though? Seems like a pretty girl like you—if you don't mind me calling you a girl—belongs down in the tourist quarter. You know what I'm—"

"It's Eddie," she said. The name came from between her lips like hot spittle.

"Eddie?"

"My man."

LaDon leaned backwards in the booth, crossed his big biceps over his chest. "Your man?" Maybe he'd just repeat what the girl said all night—that might get her out of the life. Because LaDon knew she was in the life. And she was a little girl when it came to street smarts. He knew it from the second he handed her the free drink— the way she tipped it back, drank too much before she knew how strong the bartender made it. Way they made them in The Zip Zap Bar, the girl was feeling it after the first drink, had a tingle way down in her toes by the end of the second. And she was deep into her third.

LaDon spotted their drinks on the bar, the cocktail glasses dripping in the half-light.

He stood and walked over to get the drinks, came back to the booth and shoved the girl's glass under her nose. She sipped from her straw without moving her head. Her eyes watched LaDon as she slurped, her not-so-subtle hint of a blow job. For a price, of course.

LaDon said, "Tell me about Georgia."

"Georgia?"

"The peach state," he said sipping his drink. He was feeling it in his knees and elbows. No way in hell this girl was only tipsy—she was drunk, but hiding it well.

"It's nothing to me," Ginny said.

"You were born there."

"Being born there don't make it home."

"No, it doesn't." LaDon looked around the bar, took inventory of the regular crowd. He knew most everybody in the place, and that meant Eddie—Ginny's "man"—

was outside somewhere. "Home's like a state of mind or something, a head space. Am I right?"

"Like how you feel when you walk around."

"There it is."

"I was a beauty queen."

"How'd your report card look?"

She laughed at that. "Straight A's with a B in calc."

"I'm an all-star in imperfect algebra," he said.

"You're funny too." Ginny put both elbows on the table, pursed her rouge lips.

"You were telling me about this beauty queen in Georgia. Something about straight A's and nice parents. Siblings and—"

"My sister died in a boating accident."

LaDon nodded. He saw it: A refugee of grief. Come on out to California and make your dreams come true. But don't you forget about the pimp waiting at the bus station: Eddie—steady Eddie.

How many steady Eddies are stalking bus stations in America, LaDon wondered?

Ginny kept talking. "It was an accident, but my parents...They couldn't take it. My mom sits in the den, knits all goddamn day. And my dad, he's just walking around like..." She stopped and sighed. "He's fucking catatonic."

"A what-ya-ma-call-it?"

"Don't play stupid with me," Ginny said.

LaDon grunted, ran a finger along the edge of Ginny's chin. "I'm being the devil's advocate."

"The devil has enough fucking advocates."

"Amen to that," LaDon said. He added, "I'm sorry about your sister."

Ginny shrugged, finished her drink. She set the glass

down. Her pretty eyes searched for LaDon's there in the green neon light of a Rolling Rock sign. "I'm listening to you and I'm wondering: You want me to talk the jizz out of you? Is that what this is?"

LaDon bit the insides of his mouth. He watched Ginny sit there in a dirty booth in a dirty bar, her rouge lips and drugged-out look the telltale signs of a whore's imperfect glory. He did imagine those lips on his cock, but the thought made his stomach turn—not because Ginny wasn't beautiful, but because LaDon hated to see a woman selling her body. He understood it because he understood the business of being alive. But nobody said you couldn't hate necessity.

LaDon said, "No, Ginny. I don't want you to talk the jizz out of me."

Her eyes dulled. She was thinking LaDon was like every other john she'd sucked dry. "You want to know how much then? Or do you even give a fuck?"

LaDon shifted in the booth. He groaned, stood up, and glared down at her. He crossed those big arms over his chest again and said, "I want to negotiate my price with steady Eddie."

"Who?"

"Your man," LaDon said. "Why don't you take me outside and make an introduction?"

TEN

Echo almost spit out his first taste of the charcoal-filtered vodka mixed with an off-brand energy drink. It was like tasting day-old sweat. The techno music boomed in his ears making the hair on his face tingle. Echo leaned against the glass bar—lit from below with a halogen blue light—and watched the club set wiggle their asses, wave green glow sticks at each other. He found the club a few blocks inland, while he wandered drunk from one bar to another. Twice he was denied entry by fat bouncers with facial hair. Echo wanted to bust some more heads, but a night in the drunk tank didn't suit him. He wanted a lady friend for the night, a drunk-as-fuck kind of fuck. Enter The Beachcomber—ladies techno night. Echo walked as straight as he could, kept his mouth shut in the entry line, and the bouncers didn't say shit. He did his reconnaissance first, checked out the dance floor, the bar, the washrooms and the unlocked janitorial door just outside them. You want success? You got to do your homework. Like with this thing concerning Glanson. Echo needed to do his homework on that. And he planned to. But for now he watched a bunch of chicks sliding against wannabe gangsters with mini bottles of Moet frothing in their fists.

Echo hated the music. And he hated the scene. But the scenery wasn't bad.

One girl caught his eye, a brunette in a short black dress and heels. She wore insect-eye sunglasses and a little black purse over one shoulder. She didn't dance hard like the other girls, but instead shimmied left and right to the music, her plump ass bouncing beneath thin fabric.

That's her, Echo thought. She's the one.

But he couldn't make his legs move. The vodka-energy mix was supposed to help with that. Echo found himself leaning heavy against the bar, watching the brunette and thinking more about Glanson's plan. What if, Echo started thinking, I find a way to rob Glanson and his boss? That would be a score. Talking about some *fuck you* money—yes, sir. Hoo-fucking-rah-rah. And the way Glanson kept looking around that restaurant, Echo thought he'd never see an old war buddy coming for him.

Not until it was too goddamn late.

The brunette walked over to the bar, short stepping in her high heels. She started digging into her purse. Before she came out with a credit card, Echo sidled up beside her and touched her bare elbow with two callused fingers. He had to shout through the bump-bump-bump.

"I think you look good, girl."

She swung her head toward him and her eyes showed beneath the sunglasses as the strobe lights flashed on the dance floor. She shouted back in a high-pitched, party-girl voice. "Get me a drink to prove it then."

"What do you want?"

"Top-shelf vodka martini," she said and turned to lean against the bar, stare out at the bobbing crowd. Her head bobbed with the music.

Echo waved at the bartender, leaned into the man's ear

and said, "Get me a well vodka martini for this chick. Make it strong, okay? I'll have another vodka-energy drink thing."

The bartender smirked, began to make the drinks.

Echo watched the brunette bob her head. He leaned into her ear and said, "I bet you get drinks for free all night."

She nodded. "Every night."

"What I want to know is, does it end there?"

She didn't answer until Echo paid for the drinks, handed the martini to her. She squinted at the drink, as if assessing the vodka's clarity. "It depends," she said, "if the loser who buys me a drink goes for the well vodka, even after I ask for top shelf..."

Echo said, "Nothing but the best, baby."

"I'm not your fucking baby." She stepped away from him, shimmied slightly as she got into the next song. Her short hair swung across bare shoulders and her dress moved up and down her stomach, like fabric ran across a washboard.

Echo felt a tinge in his underwear. He moved beside her. Closer. So she felt how strong he was, how much bigger than her. "Maybe you're not my baby," he said, "but you can be my bitch."

Echo knew the look that crossed her face—absolute disgust.

And it turned him on. He grabbed her elbow with one hand, gripped it so tight he knew she'd have a deep black bruise.

"Ouch, man. What the fuck? You fucking—"

"I don't like it gentle," he shouted into her ear.

She struggled against his grip, started to pull away and protest. "Get the fuck off me, man—" She dropped her drink and the glass shattered. Nobody heard it with the crashing booms of the music. "I can't fucking feel—"

"Shut the fuck up." Echo held onto the brunette, drained his drink, set the glass on the bar. He began to nudge the brunette toward the restrooms, pushing her through the crowd, cut her off saying, "You always treat me like this. We're going home. I'm sick of you dancing with other guys and treating me like—"

"I don't know this motherfucker!" Her sunglasses slipped off her nose, fell soundlessly to the floor. A few heads turned their way and the brunette struggled.

Echo screamed: "You're fucking drunk again!"

The heads turned back to the dancing crowd.

They moved into the hall, turned away from the line of women trying not to piss their pants. Echo pushed the brunette into the wall, stunned her—he saw the pain flash through her eyes.

She said, "What the fuck are you doing?"

"Be quiet and it'll be easier." They moved past the men's room, just missed a frat boy stumbling into the hallway. Echo saw the janitorial door. No cameras trained on the hallway here, at this angle. As they moved toward the door, he felt the brunette slacken, sensed the energy and fight running out of her. He thought: There it is—that's what I want, sweetie.

They reached the door. With the brunette to his left, Echo reached for the door handle. As he turned it, a blooming pain ran up his crotch, spread into his belly, seemed to come out of his throat in a gasp as thick as vomit. He went to his knees, fell on his left side. He saw the brunette running down the dark hall away from him, one of her feet bare and slapping against the cement.

Echo tried to catch his breath, curled into the fetal

position. Beside him, lying on its side, was one black high-heeled shoe. He decided right then—you can make a weapon out of anything.

Despite the pain in his crotch and the throb in his testicles, Echo grinned.

ELEVEN

LaDon walked a few steps behind Ginny, tried to stop himself from watching the smooth rise and fall of her ass. He swung his eyes up and down the dark street behind The Zip Zap Bar. Rundown houses with boards over the windows, a few missing doors where LaDon spotted the soft glow of flashlights and lanterns—drug squatters using the abandoned houses as places to shoot up. Fucking shooting galleries.

Ginny's high heels clicked on the sidewalk and she hummed to herself as they walked.

LaDon couldn't place the song, but it was somehow familiar. He thought about asking Ginny what it was, but spotted a head moving in a parked car, a dusty late model Impala with white rims. Ginny stopped for a second, started moving again without looking back at LaDon.

LaDon fell back farther, reached into his pants pocket and came out with a four-inch blade. Nothing fancy. A pocket knife made from decent steel, something he picked up on sale at Big 5. A little tool for unexpected jobs.

Ginny moved faster, the click of her heels growing more rapid. LaDon memorized the Impala's license number—IMA-PMP4—and squinted to see through the window. He saw the head turn as Ginny approached, leaned down to speak through the passenger side window. Ginny stopped, began to kneel and speak to the driver, but she stood when LaDon moved closer.

LaDon said, "No, Ginny. Not like that because—"

And she started running across the street.

The pimp, Eddie, was out of the Impala faster than LaDon anticipated. With a bulky black pistol in his hand—pointed at LaDon.

LaDon kept his blade close against his thigh, didn't have to try hard to act surprised after seeing the gun. "Yo, man. I'm just out here with my girl. You know—"

Eddie said, "She's my girl. I know that. And so do you." His hand shook holding the gun, but it was steady enough to threaten. His face was flat and pale, a smashed image of a man in the darkness. "You trying to do something to me? That what the blade's for?"

LaDon shook his head. He looked past Eddie at Ginny standing on the opposite side of the street. Her arms were crossed and one hip was cocked upward, as if she was a teenager watching boys at the mall. LaDon moved his gaze back to Eddie. "The blade's for protection," he said. "I don't know this girl—that's all."

"You're going to come out here and rob me? That what this is?"

"You're one curious motherfucker."

"I want to know what's going on, big ass fucker like you stepping to me with a knife."

LaDon watched the gun. He tried to see Eddie's eyes in the darkness. This is what you get for trying to save someone, LaDon. This is what you get. He said, "I'm not trying to get shot."

Eddie shrugged, looked across the street at Ginny. A

smile came to his face as he swung back to LaDon. "Nope, not for some girl you barely know."

"I heard that."

"You just want to play hero when it's easy, huh?"

LaDon nodded slowly. "Ginny," he said, "you go on and get out of here. Take your ass back to Georgia. You don't need to see nothing about what men like me and Eddie do."

Eddie laughed slow, pondering—what you'd expect from a hound dog.

"It's funny?" LaDon gripped his knife more tightly. His fingers were wet with sweat.

"Ginny," Eddie said, "Get your ass over here and get in the car."

Ginny walked back across the street, moved behind Eddie while her eyes stayed on LaDon. She blinked twice and clicked her heels around the front of the Impala, opened the passenger side door. She got in and slammed the door.

LaDon watched her through the back window. She stared straight ahead without moving.

"You don't know what me and Ginny got," Eddie said.

LaDon's turn to laugh. A big one too. He said loud enough for Ginny to hear: "The only thing you got with Ginny is a dead end. Giving blow jobs ain't a profession. It's torture."

Eddie turned his hand so the gun pointed at LaDon on its side. "I thought all the saints were dead," he said while moving against the Impala.

"Not this one. Go ahead and call me Saint LaDon."

Eddie put one foot on the driver's side floorboard, said, "You go and do a miracle somewhere else. Me and

Ginny got work to do. You know how it is, trying to get paid."

LaDon nodded—he knew alright.

Eddie said, "I want you to take ten steps back. I'm going to hop in and drive away. Next time I see you with one of my girls, I'll shoot you in the fucking dick."

LaDon started moving backwards, winced as Eddie slid into the Impala, started the engine. LaDon kept moving backwards as the Impala's brake lights flashed red. The engine raced and the tires chirped as Eddie sped away. Shit, man—that didn't go like I planned, now did it? As LaDon started walking back to The Zip Zap Bar the name of the tune Ginny was humming came to him: "Big Pimpin'" by Jay-Z. He shook his head as he walked, slid a thumb up and down the sharp edge of his knife.

Good thing LaDon got Eddie's license plate.

Ginny might not want saving, but she sure as fuck needed it.

TWELVE

The next day, early in the morning beneath an overcast sky, Glanson decided which dispensary he and Echo were going to knock over first. It was a sly little place off El Cajon and Thirtieth, in a strip mall next to one of those immigration paper offices. Glanson never did get what those offices did, though he imagined it was something illegal. Or, like what him and Abel were doing, close to it. This particular dispensary had a safe, but it was in the open behind the front desk and, from what Glanson observed, rarely locked. Each time Glanson entered the place and collected the cash, the safe was propped open—odd to see with the customers walking in and smelling their weed right at the front desk. Shit, they might mix it up with the smell of money.

A lot of these weed merchants—yes, let's call them merchants—understood the need for security, for precautions. But this particular guy, an ex-biker with a prominent limp and the longest beard Glanson ever saw up close, seemed to depend on his persona for security. The man, Roddie, was a nice enough fucker, but he didn't seem concerned about theft. The only reason he used Abel and Glanson was because, he told Glanson one day, he was sick of burying bags of money in his yard—it got moldy underground, especially during late spring and summer.

Roddie liked his cash crisp and clean.

Funny, Glanson liked it that way too.

He chose Roddie's dispensary for the first job when Abel got a call. They were sipping coffee in their Econoline van, waiting outside McDonald's before a long day picking up cash that was unsanctioned and untaxed by the United States government.

"This is Abel, M&J Security, how can I help you?" He rubbed his face with a pudgy hand while the voice on the other end droned. "Alright then," Abel said. "We can make the pick up early tomorrow morning. That's what I'd suggest given—" Abel rolled his eyes when the voice cut him off. "I know it. Ten in the morning then. Tomorrow. We'll be there." Abel hung up and licked his lips, shook his head. "Fucking guy thinks he's Mr. Bad Ass."

"Who's that?" Glanson tried to say it without interest, like he didn't give two shits.

"Roddie, over off Thirtieth. Says he's got a thing for his granddaughter this afternoon and he won't be in for the pickup, shutting down early."

"We can head over there now, get what he had from the rest of the week."

Abel shook his head, slurped tar-like coffee from his McDonald's cup. "Too many other pickups this morning. Roddie's stash can wait. He'll be alright."

"What's Roddie's deal anyhow?"

Abel shrugged. "Some PI friend I got said Roddie went down for meth trafficking. Did a few years, got out on good behavior. Man's in the weed business because he's trying to go legit now. Except, of course, for the money part of it." Abel slipped the van into drive and it slid out of the parking lot, headed west on the main avenue. He made a left onto Park, started south toward their first stop. "I sure as shit wouldn't fuck with Roddie."

"Maybe," Glanson said, "but 'bangers don't know that. I just wonder, all this marijuana money's got to be on the radar for somebody." He watched the city crawl by like film, thrift stores and coffee shops and pizza shacks all wedged together like misshapen bricks in a wall.

"It's on my radar," Abel said. "Why I got into the business, right?"

"You think about it and you wonder why the feds don't just legalize, get the tax funding."

Abel nodded and said, "I think about that too, but you got all the evangelicals, dumbass Christian fuckers complaining about abortion and pot. You're a congress-man or whatever and last thing you need is legal pot on your résumé. Makes your next race a real bitch."

"I guess that's it," Glanson said. He finished his coffee, bit the plastic top with sore teeth. "You know, I went overseas and fought for this country. I'll tell you the truth—I did some fucked up shit. And here I am, stand-ing in some desert with fungus growing on my balls, watching one of my buddies bleed out after some fucker made a IED from a Folgers coffee can and a clock radio, and I don't know jackshit about how democracy works. You asked me back then how a bill goes into law, I got no fucking idea. Shit, I can't tell you what the fucking stock market is. I mean, I can't describe it, teach it to a fifth grader."

Abel laughed. "You and everybody-fucking-else."

"Right, and that's fucked up. We got people killing

for shit they don't even understand."

"Look, Glanson," Abel said. "If you're going in for this anti-war crap, I don't—"

"You won't get none of that from me." Glanson bit harder into the coffee cup's lid. "I loved that mother-fucking war. I wish we had ourselves another one, place it isn't so fucking hot. All I'm saying, what I'm trying to understand, is nothing makes fucking sense. It's out there, all this stuff happening, but it doesn't make sense. Like this thing about weed. And all this money. You want the tax dollars, you got to let the banks take in the money."

Abel sighed, slowed for a right turn. They waited at a red light, heavy traffic passing them. The blinker made its slow metronome click. "Maybe if they could see it all," Abel said. "If they could see these bags of fucking money—I bet that would make some goddamn sense."

Yes-fucking-sir, Glanson thought, that would make some fucking sense. The weight of money: how could that not make fucking sense?

THIRTEEN

Through the office window—crossed by vertical steel bars—Jessie saw LaDon's Cutlass slide against the curb, jerk as he set the emergency brake, and shut down. She watched LaDon, big-looking in a black button down and pink tie, exit the car, lift his chin at a man walking toward the main avenue, and start across the street. LaDon walked like he knew people, like he was some-body for other people to know. What was that called? Swag, Jessie thought. LaDon had swag. She liked that about him, and she liked how LaDon—to this point—hadn't needed his professional knowledge. He hadn't busted any heads in Jessie's dispensary.

She hoped that was how things stayed, but Jessie wasn't foolish—she knew the risks.

When he opened the door and let himself into the waiting room, LaDon gave Jessie an inquisitive glare through the closed-circuit television camera. She buzzed him in and he poured himself some coffee and sank into his swivel chair, a bit of the liquid splashing out of his mug onto the thin office carpet. "You make this coffee? Tastes like tree bark," he said.

Jessie nodded and said, "It goes with my bite." She lifted the lid on a Tupperware container and sniffed about fifteen nuggets of weed. "Ummhmm. That's going to sell right there."

"You got a fancy name for that one too? Something that'll make her sell?"

"I'm calling it Princess Leia."

"Like fucking Star Trek?"

"Star Wars," Jessie said. "You know, you might want to brush up on pop culture."

"Tell me who won the Super Bowl." LaDon shifted in his chair, finished the coffee in one long slurp. He clanged the mug on his desk.

"Besides football, I mean." Jessie sealed the Tupperware container, moved to her computer and began to update an online menu listing for their business. Customers signed in with a password and browsed a secure database of Jessie's weed inventory. "And what was that look for?"

"What's that?"

"When you came in just now—you looked at me."

"I can't look at you?"

"Not like that."

LaDon nodded and cleared his throat. "I'm wondering how your night was with—"

"Abbie?"

"Tell me that ain't what his momma called him."

Jessie laughed and said, "His full name is Abbicus."

"Like the thing...You know." LaDon wagged a finger on each hand.

"They used to count with."

"That's it. Old school calculator. We should get one of those."

"Ha ha, LaDon. You want to count all our money with that? Go right the fuck ahead."

"Oh, hell no," LaDon said. "I'll admit it—we're making too much for that, to go old school."

Jessie stood and poured herself some coffee, leaned back against her desk, and crossed her legs. She knew LaDon had to force himself not to trace the gracious curves. "Since you asked about my night...It was nice. We drank some sparkling wine and had some sparkling conversation. Abbie is sweet. He's been through a lot."

"The fuck does that mean?"

"He was in the war."

"Okay," LaDon said. "He's on some PTSD shit, that what you're saying?"

Jessie rolled her eyes.

"You two didn't fuck?"

"LaDon, we're friends, but don't think you got a right to know who I fuck. Or who I don't."

"We're adults in this room right now, ain't we? What, I'm supposed to ask if the man made sweet love to you? Don't stand there all sexy and act like—"

"Who I fuck is my business, you jealous mother-fucker."

LaDon laughed and said, "You mess around with his thing? Do that for the man, at the very least?"

"What am I? Some tenth-grade slut?"

"You tell me, sister."

This jealousy—if that's what the fuck it was—pissed Jessie off. Another man being a goddamn grown-up baby. "You want to tell me what your fucking problem is today?"

They stared at each other. Jessie sipped her coffee. LaDon picked his thumbnails.

After a long while, he said, "I'm wondering if he knows about the plants."

"You woke up on the asshole side of the bed, didn't you?"

"Does he know? It's what I need to understand."

Jessie felt the anger bubble inside her. She breathed hard through her nose, counted to four before saying, "You must think I'm a dumb fucking bitch. Is that what you think?"

"Jessie, you know I don't—"

"Because Jessie gets a little wet and she can't help but to jeopardize our business, right? It's Jessie who has the sex problem, the fucking-everything-that-moves problem. It's me, huh?"

"Girl, I'm trying to do my—"

"I'm not your girl, LaDon." Jessie finished her coffee, set the mug down with a violent thump, and crossed her arms. "And I'm not some dumb bitch."

"I know that—"

"You think I'm going to show some guy I barely know all my thousands in marijuana grow? You think I'm that stupid, that I'm a big fucking idiot?"

LaDon held up one large hand—dared her to talk to it. "I said, 'does he know?' That's different."

"How the fuck would he know?" The muscles in Jessie's face tightened, hardened like stone.

"You have your eyes on the man the entire time he was at your place?"

"Of course."

"You didn't run and take a tinkle?"

"Don't talk to me like a child."

"Jessie, I'm doing my job here. I'm asking, did you leave Glanson alone while he was in your apartment? For any length of time?"

She watched LaDon sitting behind his desk, how he

crossed his arms casually, let his head fall on one shoulder. That was it, still looking cool even though Jessie may have fucked up. Probably did fuck up. That was LaDon's swag, the thing she liked about him most. Fuck, Jessie said to herself, fuck me. "I ran to the bathroom twice," she said. "But that's all. I wasn't gone for—"

"He knows," LaDon said. "You bet your sweet white ass—the motherfucker knows."

FOURTEEN

The Fizz Bar—hole-in-the-wall joint off El Cajon and Forty-second. Echo walked in and took a seat at the bar, deep in the neon glow of beer signs, where he could watch the entrance without seeming suspicious. It was seven in the evening and already dark outside. Echo sipped a Bud and tried to concentrate on the bulky feel of the .45 wedged in his pants, hidden beneath his loose Hawaiian shirt. It excited him to think he might use the gun tonight. At least, that's what he gathered from Glanson's voicemail: "Meet me at The Fizz Bar around seven. I got our first job worked out. We're doing it tonight. Time to get paid, motherfucker." There was a glee in Glanson's voice; it came through clear in his tone and rapid delivery. Echo got the message at a bar down in Mission Beach. He was halfway through his third Mimosa and thought, fucking crazy-ass Glanson is going through with it. And I'm on board, taking my fucking orders.

As Echo ordered a second Bud, Glanson slinked into the bar, his full-face motorcycle helmet wedged under an arm. He nodded at the bartender and a neat glass of whiskey hit the bar as he sat down next to Echo. "Hey, Ec. Good to see you." He set his helmet on the bar, slurped the whiskey. "What are you driving tonight, buddy?"

Echo swiveled on his stool, faced Glanson. "You saying you want me to drive?"

"We can't carry bags of money on a motorcycle, can we?"

Echo studied the bartender, but the man—mid-fifties and slumped like a dead plant—ignored them while he crushed ice with a meat tenderizer. "I'm in a broke-ass Honda Civic. One of the cylinders is misfiring. Runs like the piece of shit it is."

"Only you'd find a way to make a Honda run crappy."

Echo smirked. He turned back to his beer and shrugged. "I'm thinking I need a new ride."

"You make sure to get something used after tonight," Glanson said. "And nothing fancy, motherfucker. I'm talking a sedan or economy car. Put a sound system in it if you want, but nothing that'll make people look at you."

"You think I'm a dummy, Glanson?"

Glanson shook his head. He swirled his glass in a circle on the bar, ran a long fingernail in the trail of condensation it left. "I'm planning on ten grand tonight. It's not much, okay? I know that, but it's a start. It's just the first—"

"You said this was fucking gold."

"It's like anything else: You need some practice and then you hit the big motherfuckers."

"Make sure you know what the fuck," Echo said. "And how the fuck." Reconnaissance. Intelligence. Knowing what the fuck and how the fuck were essential.

Glanson pushed away from the bar. He stood and finished his drink.

Echo said, "We doing it right this minute?"

"Why wait?"

Glanson stared at him with those crazy-sane eyes.

They drove by once and Glanson pointed out the strip mall. It was right on the street with a small alcove and courtyard, four or five shops facing each other across the cement cutout. Echo noted signs for an immigration service, a watch repair shop, and a DUI attorney's office. Lot of money in that racket, Echo knew. Especially in a resort town where every hour was a happy hour. Echo flipped a U-turn at the next stoplight, headed south on a side street before they passed the strip mall again. He parallel parked on a residential street about two blocks from the main avenue.

Echo pulled out his .45, chambered a round. "What if this motherfucker happens to be there?"

"He won't," Glanson said. He examined his own gun, a 9mm, shoved it back into his waistband. "I wish like hell we had a shotgun with us."

"Smart," Echo said. "Two war vets strolling down the street with a loaded scattergun. You aren't trying to get me locked up, are you?"

"If the place had parking, we could just—"

"What, smile for the closed-circuit cameras?" Echo sighed and pinched the bridge of his nose. "I'm saying, this ain't fucking Eye-Rack, Glanson. It's America, buddy. We do this and we're—"

"Only person who's going to give a shit is this guy Roddie. That's all this is: pissing one lone motherfucker off. Nothing more and nothing less." Glanson sneezed, wiped his nose with the back of his hand.

Echo wasn't sure but he said, "I hope you're right."

* * *

The front of the strip mall area was lit by two halogen lamps high on the building. The beige walls looked yellow in the light and Echo was aware of how passersby could see two figures slinking beside the building. Traffic was still heavy this late in the evening but he knew that while they were likely to be seen, they were unlikely to be noticed. Echo followed Glanson as he moved into the dark courtyard. None of the offices was occupied—all the windows were dark.

Glanson stopped for a moment, listened to the traffic and chopper noise booming through the city. He shrugged and moved quickly to the door of the dispensary.

Echo read the block letters on the door over Glanson's shoulder. They were the kind you buy from a hardware store and stick on yourself: *CalMed Solutions: Herbal Remedies.* He shook his head and laughed without noise. Nothing like a solution for your remedy, or a remedy for your solution. He whispered to Glanson, "You going to pick the lock?"

Glanson shook his head. He removed the 9mm from beneath his shirt and fired one booming shot slightly higher than the door handle.

Echo's ears rang. This crazy motherfucker—Echo couldn't believe it. "What the fuck, man?"

Glanson slammed a boot into the door and it crashed inward, splintered across the carpeted floor of the office.

"Glanson!" It didn't matter if anybody heard them now. Echo imagined the shots fired call going over the police scanner. "We need to get the fuck out of here!"

Glanson didn't listen. He moved across the office, through an open door to a glassed-in counter and large desk—like in a bank—and crouched near a dark shape about the size of a refrigerator.

Echo leaned into the doorway, looked for cameras in the corners of the room. He saw nothing. Behind him, the courtyard was still empty, the flash and hum of traffic whipping by on the street. Fuck it, Echo thought. It's like walking into an ambush. Or whatever the fuck. He was inside a moment later, leaning over Glanson and watching as the safe came open. "You knew the combination? How the fuck did you—"

"Man's lazy," Glanson said. "He doesn't lock it, just acts like he does."

"Jesus." There were several small stacks of bills in Ziploc bags. Beside that, Echo saw several Tupperware boxes filled and stacked atop each other. "What's all that?"

Glanson started stacking the money in a reusable shopping bag. On its sides, the bag said: *I hope you fill my tummy too!* Glanson said, "That's all the man's weed. It's his inventory."

"You think we should take that?"

Glanson finished packing the money, thought for a second. "I see no reason to ruin the man's livelihood. Plus, we got to resell the shit." He hefted the shopping bag with his left hand. The gun dangled from the other. "We're good with this, I think."

Echo didn't give a shit. He knew the cops must be on the way. He was certain someone on the street or in the nearby neighborhood reported the blast from the 9mm. "Let's get the fuck out of here then." Echo turned to lead Glanson out of the office.

A shadow appeared in the doorway. This particular shadow had a beard. Echo lifted the .45 and aimed.

From the doorway, Roddie said, "You dumb mother-fuckers."

A thing Echo learned in the war: You don't think about what you have to do. You just do it. When it comes down to you or somebody else, you just do it. It isn't a choice—you let your instincts choose for you. Instincts never lie. And Echo's instincts told him to squeeze the trigger. Not once, mind you, but three times. And his vision tunneled as he saw the shadow in the doorway lurch sideways, grab the doorframe, stumble toward him. Echo fired once more, a shot that entered the top of the man's head. He fell a few feet from Echo and lay still.

The sound of the gunshots rang through Echo's head, died after a moment—he thought of church bells for some odd reason. He let the gun fall to his side and breathed heavily into the darkness. The room smelled of damp plant life and dirty coins. He felt Glanson move to his side.

Glanson said, "You still got it, baby. I have to admit: I fucking wondered."

Echo didn't speak.

Glanson stepped over the big man lying dead on the floor and moved through the doorway. He turned and motioned for Echo to follow. "Let's go, buddy. We got to get the fuck out of here."

Glanson moved into the dark courtyard, rounded a corner and moved out of sight along the street. Echo looked down once more at the dead man. He heard the police chopper somewhere nearby. Sirens started a few blocks north. The traffic kept moving, ceaseless and insistent. It didn't surprise Echo to know a man could die—a man could be killed—and nothing in the world stopped or paused. It all kept moving. The .45 felt like a toy in his hand. He smiled and thought of water guns, how he used to spray paint them black when he was a kid. So they looked real.

Okay, buddy. You got to get out of here. The sirens sounded closer, right on top of him. Echo shook his head. He looked around the office once more, didn't see any cameras. I'm fine. Nobody but Glanson can put me here. And he wouldn't dare. Not to an old war buddy. Okay, buddy. You got to get out of here. Sure, Echo thought. Sure. Sure. He nodded. He stepped over the body, moved into the courtyard. The night air was cool and thin. Echo walked through the darkness, slipped the warm gun into his waistband, covered it with his flowing shirt.

Be cool, Echo told himself. Be easy as fuck.

He sauntered along the sidewalk, turned the next corner and saw Glanson waiting for him there.

The bag of money swung in pendulum from Glanson's hand. "C'mon, Ec. What the fuck?"

"I'm with it," Echo said. "Don't you worry about me."

They moved down the street, two loping shadows in the darkness. The police chopper crossed high above and, a few blocks behind Echo and Glanson, the sirens grew louder, whined like frantic hyenas. This night air feels good, Echo thought. It's nice.

He didn't think about the dead man.

No—he thought about the money. Echo wanted to know: How much did we get?

FIFTEEN

LaDon, pink tie still tight around his thick neck, sat drinking a Sazerac in the lounge at the Bayside Hyatt. The place smelled of starched collars and spreadsheets. Fucking business travelers. LaDon was waiting for Jessie to get back from the ladies' room. They were going to order appetizers. LaDon wanted those little hot dogs with umbrellas sticking out of them, but Jessie was partial to the fried calamari. Full of fancy tastes, that woman. Above the couch where LaDon reclined, a television set was tuned to the local news—channel ten, he thought. LaDon couldn't hear the sound while the jazz trio played in front of the window looking out on the bay and the Coronado Bridge. But when they stopped for a break, he caught the lady newscaster mentioning illegal dispensaries and something about...Wait, what?

She said, "Homicide detectives are looking for any information about last night's slaying in the Mid-City area. The victim is a war veteran, a former US Marine, and, according to investigators, was running an illegal marijuana dispensary. It appears theft was a factor in the murder."

They ran a shot of a dumpy strip mall from across the street, all the traffic zooming past for color and movement. The next shot was closer on the strip mall and showed yellow crime scene tape stretched across a doorway. After all that, they flashed the number for Crimestoppers.

The next story was about dogs surfing down south. A hell of a lot more pleasant, if you asked LaDon. Jessie crossed in front of him a moment later and sank into the couch, picked up a menu, and started reading through it.

"You order yet?"

"I'm waiting for you."

The jazz trio started up again and Jessie wrinkled her nose. "Old people music," she said, glancing at the television.

"Dispensary got hit in Mid-City," LaDon said. "Owner got dead and the money got gone."

Jessie pulled her head from the menu, gave LaDon a deadpan stare.

"You think I'm fucking with you?"

"They say who it was?"

"No names came out but it looked like a planned thing. From what I could tell, at least."

A confused expression crossed Jessie's face; her eyebrows got uneven and wrinkles deepened on her forehead. "What are you thinking?"

LaDon shrugged, not knowing what to say.

"Should we hire another person, run all-night security?"

"We only got M&J coming twice a week?"

Jessie nodded. Twice a week wasn't enough time for her to flirt with Abbie, but they weren't doing enough volume to make the money pickup a daily thing. Not yet, at least.

"We either make that an everyday thing," LaDon

said, "Or I'm going to have to take the money home every night. We can't leave it there—we got every Tom, Dick, and Harry coming in to buy their weed. Could be, one of those dumb fucks got an idea about how to get easy money."

"You think it was a stoner? Really?" Jessie waved the waitress over and said, "Can we get a plate of calamari? And my friend here likes those little wieners, the ones with the umbrellas. We'll get another round of drinks, too." The waitress moved off through the lounge chairs and couches.

"Maybe some gangbangers," LaDon said. "Could be that—they know how."

"Maybe you could ask around?"

LaDon sat up in the soft couch, played with his tie for a bit. "I might run it by a few people, but we can't leave our inventory or cash in the office. Next thing we know, we're out on our asses."

Jessie finished her white wine and said, "We still have our savings. With M&J."

LaDon wasn't so sure about that now. Yeah, they had a contract with the security service, but it wasn't legit. It wasn't insured. M&J was on the same legal ground as the dispensary business. They were running security and picking up money in open violation of federal law.

LaDon bit one side of his bottom lip. "I'm thinking we need to start dealing with our own money, washing it, the whole thing. I mean, how far you really think we can trust those two?"

"Fuck no," Jessie said. "Abbie's not like that. And neither is his boss. I shouldn't have let him see our grow. Fine, you're right about that. But they're not—"

"You going to call the cops on them if anything does happen? You think robbery and homicide is going to work a B&E for you?"

Jessie didn't respond. Instead, she smiled at the waitress setting their drinks on the low table before them. Jessie thanked her and picked up LaDon's Sazerac, tried to hand it to him.

As LaDon reached for his second drink, Jessie let the glass fall.

"What the fuck—"

"That's what you get."

LaDon stood. He set the glass on the table, wiped liquid from his crotch area. "Jessie, damn you. Why'd you go and do that? These are my going out slacks, man."

"You keep talking to me like you're my pimp."

LaDon shook his head, couldn't help thinking about Ginny from the previous night. And Steady Eddie, her nice little pimp with the pistol. "I'm not trying to hurt your feelings," LaDon said. "I'm just worried is all. That okay with you?"

"Last I heard," Jessie said, "you can worry without being a chauvinist pig."

LaDon sat down again, waved the waitress over for a new drink. "I hope you plan to pay for that drink. You invited me out for cocktails, remember that."

Jessie shrugged him off, leaned back in the couch with her arms behind her head. "You know what? Let's cancel our order. I want to go some place with class."

LaDon didn't say anything, but in his head he was thinking: thanks for coming to your senses.

SIXTEEN

Abel piloted the white Econoline van into the grocery store parking lot, set up so they were facing the small dispensary off Market Street. Another one the cops hadn't hooked up on, run by a rasta with an MBA, if you can believe that shit. He rolled down his window and Glanson did the same. Both men lit cigarettes and sat there smoking and scowling.

Abel scratched behind his head and said, "It's no good for business, this thing with Roddie's place. It's going to start people asking questions about us."

"See," Glanson said, "I think the opposite." He wanted to smile at the thought of Roddie collapsing into his own office, a bullet going through his head. Fucking Echo, man. Shit, that was why Glanson pulled Echo in. He knew Echo's instincts, his moral composition.

"How's that?"

"Roddie called off the pickup and he got hit. We make the point—you need us every single day if you want your money safe. If you want to keep it. Every fucking day."

Abel sighed and coughed a few times out the window. He spat, ran a finger under his seatbelt. "And we get two more trucks, four more guys. Start making it mandatory we come each day." He tilted his head from side to side. "It could work, but—"

"We're the only game in town," Glanson said. "Me and you."

"I need to get more storage units. A big safe we can put in there. And we're going to have to make arrangements with the storage facility manager…"

"Some time, we're going to need our own facility. A round-the-clock guard detail."

"You're talking a fucking bank," Abel said.

Glanson opened his door, climbed out with one hand on the reassuring shape of his gun. He shut the door and leaned into the open window. "Look, Abel. This is shit we know. It's a fucking goldmine, man. You're an innovator." He left Abel sitting in the driver's seat, chain smoking Marlboros and plotting his next stage of entrepreneurship. Glanson crossed the street and entered the dispensary, a small shop between a record store and a barber.

"Yo, man. Mr. Security. I been waiting for you."

The rasta man's place smelled like cinnamon incense and weed all mixed together. He was a large man with flat features, a broad belly spilling out of a loose green t-shirt with a marijuana leaf on the front. His dreadlocks hung past his shoulders, twisted like an octopus on one side of his head. Bob Marley posters on the walls, strings of different colored beads hanging from the ceiling. The place also sold tie-dyed shirts and serapes with Marley's face on them.

There were no customers present and Glanson approached the counter. "How you doing, Sammy? Haven't seen you since last week." Sammy went into a back room; Glanson knew he was opening the safe. "How's business, buddy?"

"Booming, man," Sammy said from the back room. "It's taking off, man. I'm asking now, how can I get you here twice a week?"

There we go, Glanson thought. "Let me get you on the schedule. What days you want?"

"Tuesday and Friday," Sammy said walking in with a small gray duffel bag. He set the bag on the counter. "We got thirty thou in here. Lot of small bills."

"Jesus H.," Glanson said.

Sammy shrugged. "Me people love the bud, man."

"I can see that." Glanson hefted the bag, swung it over his shoulder. He peered outside and spotted Abel still smoking in the van. He wondered if Abel had the vision required to make real money. Glanson had the vision—you hit some of these dispensaries and drive up demand. Next thing you know, you're indispensable. To the dispensaries. And Glanson understood they had a limited window of time. The feds were going to go after the tax revenue, Glanson was certain of that. He turned and faced Sammy. "You hear about the Mid-City thing?"

"What's that?" Sammy was rolling a joint for himself.

"Murder, pal. A dispensary right off El Cajon."

"No kidding?"

"Owner got killed. And they took the money."

Sammy nodded. He reached beneath the counter and came out with a sawed-off shotgun. "They can try it, man. I guess they can try it."

"They hit the man after business hours," Glanson said. "He just happened to come in for something. Bad luck, you know?"

Sammy studied the shotgun in his hands. "I got the safe back there."

"A safe can be broken, Sammy. You've seen the movies."

"What are you saying?"

Glanson said, "You better make it three days a week, protect your investment."

"Man, you belong in the government. You know that?"

Glanson laughed. He lifted the shirt sleeve on his right arm, revealed the tattoo of the M16. "I already did my time for Uncle Sam."

"Shit, we all do our time somehow. You make it two days a week." Sammy hid the shotgun beneath the counter again. "I can handle the other five. Know what I mean?"

"Suit yourself, pal," Glanson said. He exited the dispensary, looked both ways and quickly crossed the street. As he threw the gray duffel into the rear seat of the van, Glanson thought: more fear—that's what these weed-purveying motherfuckers need. More fucking fear.

SEVENTEEN

Frita's Soul Food off the 52, out in Lemon Grove—LaDon stared out the window at his Cutlass gleaming in the daylight. He chewed some pulled pork and Carolina-style BBQ, chased it with a beer. Didn't much care for thick sauce. LaDon liked that Carolina-style because it made his tongue tingle.

Across the table from LaDon, scratching his unwashed head, Moonie Sykes bit into a hush puppy and smacked his lips, sucked air between his teeth. "Man, that's some good stuff."

"Best in the city," LaDon said. "Me bringing my boy Moonie out for a lunch, huh?"

Moonie looked at him with squinted eyes. "Real nice of you, LaDon, but what the fuck you want from me? You know I'm in a program, that I'm off the streets."

LaDon shrugged, sipped more beer. "But you still hear things, huh?"

Moonie sighed, dropped a hush puppy into his paper tray. He leaned back in his chair and shook his head. "Here I am thinking you missed me."

"Oh, Moonie—I did miss you, brother. You know I miss you."

"I'm telling you, I'm not up with the same crowd."

"I'm saying you hear things, though. Tell you what: I'm going to ask a question. Tell me if you can tell me. If you can't tell me, shit, you got yourself some free BBQ."

Moonie said, "Nothing fucking free out here."

LaDon held up his hands, like he was about to get robbed. "I'm not asking you to rat on anybody. I'm just wondering," he lowered his hands to the table, "if you heard anything about that homicide in Mid-City. The dispensary thing."

"Oh, right," Moonie said. "Because you're in that business."

"New thing I got going."

Moonie nodded. He ran a dirty thumbnail across his teeth, tried to pick out a tendril of pork. "With that white girl, nice-looking one?"

"That don't matter, Moonie."

"Okay." He bit his bottom lip. "Way I heard it, the kill looked like a hit."

LaDon smirked, looked around the restaurant for eavesdroppers. Nope—bunch of people chowing down on BBQ, getting fat and happy. "The fuck you mean, a hit?"

Moonie touched his chest in three places, close together. "Guy got done by a pro. Homicide dicks are surprised at the entry wounds, thinking the head shot was overkill. Funny word, you know, given the circumstances."

"You're saying the shots were close together. Someone who had training did it."

Moonie nodded.

"How you know this?"

"My boy went down for possession the other night. He's sitting in booking, waiting on his bail bondsman, fucking cops are shooting off at the mouth. I ain't saying it's for real, but this ain't the kind of man can make that shit up." Moonie pointed to his temple. "Not all the way there, you know?"

LaDon could buy that, maybe. "Something else," he said. "You know a pimp goes by the name Eddie, runs girls out of Southeast?"

"Black girls or white girls?"

"White girls."

"That's Eddie Money. Came up in Chula Vista, white boy who thinks he's Chicano."

LaDon shook his head in surprise. "Eddie Money? Like the rock star?"

Moonie laughed. His yellow teeth showed across the table. His mouth was slick with BBQ. "I don't know, LaDon. You expect a white boy to come up with a good street name?"

"I mean…Shit."

"You might find him around Zeta's, that old taco place on Forty-Second."

"I drive by there sometimes," LaDon said.

"Careful with it. Eddie carries a piece, likes to wave it around."

LaDon nodded at that. "Believe me, I know. I ran into the man the other night. Glad I'm still breathing, heavy as it is."

"What, you got something for a girl?" Moonie coughed and cleared his throat. "I thought you liked to play the field, run around on the weekends."

"It's not that. It's just, she don't belong here."

"That's Eddie alright. He like that All-American look."

LaDon wanted to know about Eddie, but he kept going back to this thing about the dispensary murder.

"Tell me this again, Moonie. You're saying this dispensary thing, it was a hit? Why the fuck is a pro going to hit a guy at a place like that? You do him at home, or somewhere he can't get at you. Not some place of business, out in the open like that."

Moonie raised his thick eyebrows. "I didn't say it was a hit. I said, it looked like a fucking hit." Moonie tapped his chest three times like he did before. "Man got done by a pro. That don't mean he's somebody important, running around waiting to get done."

Now that, LaDon thought, made sense. He watched Moonie shove two more hush puppies into his mouth. The man looked like a zombie from a post-apocalypse film, always chewing with his mouth open. So the Mid-City thing was professional—there's some motherfuckers out there who are onto the money. They know where it's at, and they want to get it. Matter of fact, murder ain't a thing compared to the money. He said, "I guess I see it."

"What's that?" Crumbs flew from Moonie's mouth.

"How a man who knows what he's doing might start sticking up pot shops."

"Takes a lot of balls to be a stick-up man."

"Maybe," LaDon said, "or it takes a dumb shit with training." LaDon liked his thinking on this. He liked seeing an angle that nobody else saw. For some reason, that got LaDon going. He stared out the window at his gold Cutlass, thought again about the shotgun hidden in the trunk. Still loaded. Ready for action. Professional, huh? Somebody who knows what the fuck he's doing.

Who could that be, LaDon? Who the fuck could that be?

There was only one name bouncing around in LaDon's head.

EIGHTEEN

Echo followed Glanson from outside his apartment complex, a series of rundown gray buildings that reminded Echo of the barracks at Camp Lejeune. Eight in the morning, Glanson stumbled through the dead grass in the courtyard, hopped on his motorcycle, and sped off without checking his mirrors. Echo had followed Glanson home the night after they robbed and killed the biker. Echo wanted to know more about Glanson—what he was doing with the money and with his days. The money they stole—well, Echo's half—was still in the trunk of his shitty Honda, hidden beneath a bunch of dirty beach towels.

On the freeway, it was difficult to stay close behind Glanson. He rode the crotch rocket like the Japanese engineers intended—ninety miles per hour and flat out fucking crazy. Echo swerved from lane to lane without using his blinker, hoped all the highway patrol officers were eating donuts and talking football. He saw Glanson dart between two semi-trucks, take an exit for downtown. Echo followed and they turned into a third-class strip mall a few miles from the airport. As Echo parallel parked a few blocks from where Glanson was backing in his motorcycle, a 727 roared overhead—scared the shit out of Echo. Maybe he was jumpy after the other night. What Echo sort of felt, a little bit, was guilt. But not guilt for the dead man, the man he killed. Guilt because he didn't have guilt about the dead man. The same thing happened to him in Eye-Rack. Matter of fact, the Corps shrink said it was more common than Echo might think. Never did tell Echo what to do about it, but fuck it.

He didn't have to wait long before he saw Glanson and a burly guy with a shaved head come out of a window-less office. They walked through the strip mall's small parking lot and climbed into a white van. The burly guy steered the van onto the freeway and Echo followed. First, they stopped at a McDonald's and sat there shoot-ing the shit. They left there and stopped at a couple dis-pensaries in the Mid-City area, each time Glanson going into the place with a hand on his gun. He always came out with a gray or black duffel bag, his head on a swivel. The burly guy kept the van running and they left with-out drawing attention to themselves. Echo knew they didn't see him because they never tried to lose the tail— it was all business for Glanson and his boss. The last place they stopped was downtown, a rasta shop with a big fat dude talking to Glanson. At least, that's what Echo could see through the window.

By this time he was parked in the same lot as the van, confident he wouldn't be seen because—and this was fucking certain—these two weren't much for security or precaution. Echo imagined they were arrogant because they were ex-soldiers and they had guns. These two things together will do it every time. Echo knew that from his Eye-Rack contract work. Was even guilty of it himself. And, sure enough, Glanson left the rasta shop and swaggered across the street, a gray duffel bag swinging from his hand. Fucking amateur, Echo thought, and laughed.

What Echo was waiting for, hoping for, was for M&J Security to do a money drop.

He got his wish.

The van merged onto the south 805, exited about ten miles later. Echo followed the van through light traffic until it turned into an industrial section. He hung back, pulled the Honda into a closed down auto shop lot, watched as the van's driver punched a security code into a gate box and drove through a sliding door—it was a run-of-the-mill storage facility.

Alright then, Echo thought. This is where they keep the money.

It was kind of funny. Simple. Smart. But funny, too.

Leave it to some combat vets to think up a scheme like this. They had to have a safe—Echo couldn't fathom they weren't using a safe. But he thought back on the day, how casual Glanson was with the money, walking into the places and strolling out like a customer.

Nope, he thought, they don't have a safe. At least, not for all the money.

Some, sure. But not all.

About forty-five minutes later, Echo watched the van come back through the gate, make a right turn, and drive past him. He ducked while the van passed, waited until the engine noise faded, and checked his rearview mirror. The van made a quick left. They were gone.

Now what?

Echo pulled the Honda forward, parked on the street outside the storage facility. In front, there was a small office and, like he thought, a young guy with a goatee and a ponytail at the front desk. Hourly employee. He had the look.

At seven-thirty, the clerk lurched outside, locked the office, and punched a code on a panel beside the door. The alarm. He walked across the parking lot and got into the last car there, a blue Jimmy with big mud tires and bashed-to-shit side panels. The truck started up right away, and it sounded pretty good. Better man than me, Echo told himself.

He followed the Jimmy on surface streets for about fifteen minutes. They passed through a few immigrant neighborhoods, a Westfield Shopping Center, and reached a stretch of porn shops and shitty cocktail lounges. Signs advertised Keno and beer-and-shot specials. The Jimmy swung into one of the lounge parking lots, a place called Gina's, and the clerk parked the car and went inside. Yes, Echo figured, I can work with this son of a bitch. No doubt about that.

Before he went into Gina's, Echo opened his trunk, found his money, and counted out three crisp one-hundred-dollar bills. He figured that should about do it.

Gina's catered to iron workers, down-on-their-luck contractors, and administrative assistants with wide hips and too much eye shadow. Echo didn't mind the place though. It was familiar. He took a seat two spots over from his target at the bar and ordered Crown and Coke.

Strong. And in a smudged glass to boot. Classy as fuck.

On his second drink, he looked over at ponytail and said, "You want another?" The man was drinking Seagram's and Seven in a short glass.

"Damn right," ponytail said.

Echo nodded at the bartender and slid over one stool. He offered his hand. "Name's Jimmy, what's yours?"

"No shit? I drive a Jimmy."

"That yours outside? I saw that when I came in. Hope it runs better than it looks." Echo smiled to show he was playing.

Ponytail took Echo's hand and shook it. "Drives like a tank," he said. "My name's Elvis."

"No shit?"

"Like the singer," Elvis said. "My daddy was a fan."

"Weren't we all," Echo said. The drinks arrived and they clinked glasses. Echo decided to get right to it. He figured Elvis for a no-nonsense kind of man. Liked to hear shit straight up. "Look, Elvis, didn't I see you over at eh..." He snapped his fingers. "That storage place, right?"

"Safe & Secure," Elvis said. "That's me. I don't remember you. You have a unit there?"

"Not yet," Echo said. "And, look..." He checked around the bar but nobody was paying them any attention. "I don't want a unit either."

"Okay..."

Echo slapped a hundred on the bar, slid it toward Elvis. "There's two guys in a white van have a unit, come by every couple of days. I'm hoping you could let me know which unit they have."

Elvis looked at the money, raised his eyebrows. He shrugged it off, sipped his drink.

Echo slid another hundred across the bar. "C'mon, buddy."

"Units, plural," Elvis said.

"Alright. How about you give me those numbers? And the gate code, too."

Elvis sat there in stunned silence. He raised his eyebrows once more.

Echo delivered the final hundred-dollar bill.

Elvis said, "Not just today. I want three hundred every week. Or I tell them what you look like."

Echo nodded. He didn't plan on waiting a week, but sure. Whatever you want, motherfucker. "Sounds fair," he said. "I'm just looking for a little information is all—nobody gets hurt."

Elvis grabbed a cocktail napkin off the bar, pulled a blue pen from his shirt pocket, and started writing. The expression on his face said he wasn't too sure about the nobody-gets-hurt part.

Funny, Echo wasn't sure either.

NINETEEN

Jessie watched LaDon cross the street with that trade-mark swag. She was pissed. He was three hours late and she'd already sold to a few creeps with face tattoos.

When LaDon entered the dispensary, Jessie said, "I guess you come and go as you please."

LaDon sauntered to his desk, reclined in his chair and stared at her.

"You have anything to say for yourself? I've had a bunch of weirdos in here and I'm lucky—"

"Your main squeeze might be the one who did the Mid-City place," LaDon said.

Jessie stopped right there. A lump formed in her throat and she crossed her arms. "I understand if you don't like my guy, but you don't have to run his name through shit. Just tell me what the fuck you think." She didn't like the look on LaDon's face; it was the one Jessie saw when he pounded a skinny meth head down at The Zip Zap Bar a few months back. Jessie remembered LaDon watching with that serious face as the meth head cussed out the bartender and tried to slap the waitress's ass. LaDon couldn't have that—the meth head got himself a caved cheekbone and a realigned nose. That's what happened when LaDon got serious.

"What I think, I think your boy got himself an idea. And he acted on it."

"You're jealous."

"He's getting a piece of that ass? Yeah, I'm jealous. But that's not what this is."

Jessie felt heat in her face. "He seems like a nice guy."

"And he's an ex-Marine."

"So the fuck what?" Jessie shook her head and gave LaDon her mad-as-hell stare. "He's protecting our money. Why the fuck would he rip off—"

LaDon cut her off. "Who else knows where to get the money? Who else knows how to put three shots into a man right here?" LaDon tapped his chest. "And do it so close you need a goddamn microscope to see the difference?"

Jessie's mouth tasted dry. No—this couldn't be the truth. "LaDon, I respect that you're trying to figure this out. That you're trying to protect us."

"What I been doing all morning. Doing it in a soul food joint while an addict named Moonie licks his fucking chops. Paid out of my own pocket."

"Do you want to expense it?"

"Right," LaDon said. "And I'll write it off this year—that's fucking funny."

"Abbie's been nothing but trustworthy since we started this thing. You know that, LaDon. If they were going to rip us off, they would have already done it. And what about the ten grand you're washing through The Zip Zap Bar? I'd be more worried about getting ripped off that way."

LaDon swiveled his chair, shook his head. "We'll get the money washed."

"And what's the fucking fee?" The muscles in Jessie's

cheeks flexed.

"Ten percent to start. Eight the more money we can get in—"

"That's highway robbery," Jessie said. She stood and walked to the window, peered outside at the light foot traffic—a bunch of workmen in orange vests and white hard hats passed on the sidewalk. "Ten percent, up in fucking smoke."

"It's what it costs to do business," LaDon said. He stood and walked round the desk, poured himself some cold coffee. "And we're talking about something different here. We're talking about a dead man. In case you forgot, there's no money on the other side. At least, I doubt there is."

Jessie sighed. "No. There isn't. But, you know—"

"What if it's him?"

"Abbie didn't kill anybody," Jessie said. "I promise you."

"You plan on asking him?"

Jessie rolled her eyes. "If it helps you sleep at night."

LaDon nodded slowly, sipped from his coffee. "When you two getting together again?"

Jessie turned back to the window, looked out at the overcast gray sky, tried to find the sun hidden behind a deep wash of cloud cover. "Tonight," she said. "And since you're jealous—I plan on fucking him."

LaDon didn't have shit to say to that.

TWENTY

Glanson pounded on Jessie's apartment door, stood there with his hands in his pockets.

When she opened the door, Glanson got warm from his forehead down to his toes. She was wearing the same green slip as when he first visited her, but her hair was pulled up high on her head and showed the smooth and creamy nape of her neck. She smiled at him and led him into the kitchen. Glanson tried to act cool, but inside he was hot as baked beans.

She said, "You want a beer? I'm having white wine." She lifted a glass from the counter, took a long sensuous sip—like she was drinking from the fountain of youth.

"I'll have a beer, sure."

She handed him a can from the fridge and he popped the top, sipped while trying to keep his eyes on hers. Difficult. Jessie had pretty eyes, but she had nice tits and even better legs. He gulped.

"You see something you like?" She leaned back against the counter, one hip tilted.

Glanson cleared his throat. "I see something I want."

"That's good, but are you the kind of man who takes what he wants?"

Now he met her eyes with his, thought how to respond.

After another sip of beer, he said, "I've had to take every-thing I ever got."

Jessie said, "I know how that is." A drop of wine ran out of her lips, down her chin, dripped onto one bare foot.

Glanson saw the wine run off her face and took a step toward her. Lick that trail, man. "It gets down to one thing," he said. "It's when you find that what you want, shit, it's actually a thing you need. Like, you got to have it or the world's going to burn."

"Sounds like you'd make a good therapist." Jessie licked her lips.

Glanson chuckled. He could smell her as he got closer; she was all pears and grapes and sex tones. "That, or a world conqueror."

"I got something you can conquer." She laughed so hard that she almost didn't get it out.

Glanson laughed too. "You're so corny."

"I'm turned on is what I am."

"Horny?"

"Yeah."

And then his hands were on her and they clung together like Velcro, shuffled awkwardly out of the kitchen, down the hallway. Jessie tripped and Glanson caught her. She let a *whoo* sound come out of her throat and pushed her teeth into his bottom lip. Glanson tasted blood and sucked on Jessie's tongue. She moaned. Into the bed-room. He pushed her hard onto the bed and her slip moved across her waist, up into her belly. He unbuckled his pants, kicked off his boots.

"C'mon, Abbie. C'mon."

"Let me get this off."

Jessie ran her hand between her legs, moaned.

"Goddamn," he said. "Goddamn." His pants went to the carpet and he stepped out of them, joined her on the bed in his boxers, moved between her legs. Glanson started dry humping her, smiled at the little oohs and aahs coming out, the hip thrusts she gave back to him. And Glanson went from warm to hot, to steaming. He flipped her over, dry humped her ass until she laughed hysterically. "I'm ready to get inside you," he said.

Jessie bucked and flipped back over. "Okay, okay. C'mon then, Abbie. C'mon then."

He pressed against her again, bit her right earlobe.

"Fucking give it to me!" Her fingernails dug into Glanson's back, ran down to his ass. "C'mon, Abbie! Take it out! Get it in me!" Her hands moved to his front, into his underwear.

Glanson flinched slightly. Fuck it, man. Fuck it. He moved into her again, felt her thumb and index finger nip his thing, enclose it. He wanted to explode...And then he heard her voice.

"Oh."

"What? What?" Glanson let off her, came up onto his elbows. Afraid to look at her. Fuck it, man. Fuck it. He met her eyes. "What is it?" Her fingers pried at him, searched.

"I'm sorry," she said. "Is this...is this it?" Her thumb and index finger pinched, pulled. "This is all there is, all you got? I'm sorry...I've never—"

"Fuck it, man." Glanson lifted himself from the bed, yanked his underwear back to his hips. He tried to hide his tiny hard-on with a hand—not a difficult task. "Fuck it," he said again.

"I'm sorry," she said and yanked her slip back down over her wet vagina. "Jesus."

Glanson slipped his pants on, started to shove a foot into a boot. "I never should have—"

"I mean, I'm sorry."

"Don't be. Fuck it. I never should have, you know…" He was out the door.

Jessie heard the front door slam. She tied her hair back into a bun and sat cross-legged on the bed. Small. Jesus. So fucking small. Jessie looked at her hand, made the motion of pinching something tiny between thumb and index finger.

She shrugged.

And then she started laughing.

TWENTY-ONE

The security man—Abbicus Glanson—came out of Jessie's apartment faster than LaDon expected. He watched as Glanson jogged down the stairs and damn near sprinted to his motorcycle. Look at that. A two-minute man and he walks around with a nine and a smile. That served the motherfucker right. All these tough guys walking around didn't add up—LaDon knew a good many were frauds. A hunch told him: Glanson's the biggest fraud there is.

LaDon followed the motorcycle onto University Avenue, a few blocks south. Glanson turned east and moved with traffic, careful not to draw the attention of the numerous patrol cars in the area. LaDon hung back, kept his eye on the one taillight as it turned south again and pulled into a strip mall. LaDon followed, parked near the street, and watched Glanson latch his helmet to a lock on the bike's frame.

The strip mall was a rundown collection of blue-roofed buildings. An Asian market. A dollar store. A Hometown Buffet on the corner. Glanson walked toward the restaurant, looked over his shoulder and scanned the parking lot before entering.

Alright then, LaDon told himself. Man must be meeting somebody. Okay. So what are you going to do? LaDon exited his Cutlass and moved slowly through the full parking lot. It was dark but LaDon knew, as a big man, he was easily spotted. He hunched over and stuck out his belly, peered out with one eye. He made it to the closest row of cars next to the restaurant and stooped behind a battered gray pickup truck. He smelled cigarettes, two restaurant employees in stained aprons smoking near an emergency exit. LaDon scanned the restaurant's front window, looking in on a long line of family-sized booths. After five minutes or so, Glanson slid into a booth and started shoveling food into his mouth. He chewed fast, agitated. After a few minutes, he stood and carried his tray back for a second helping. Got back, slid into the booth, and ate slower. Thirty minutes later, as LaDon was thinking maybe Glanson was just out for dinner, another man slid into the booth.

Who the fuck are you?

The two men talked for a few minutes, the new guy chewing hard and fast.

LaDon didn't know what he hoped to see out in the parking lot, but then the new guy lifted his arm to wave down an employee and LaDon saw it: A thick tattoo—a gun from the looks of it.

Then LaDon had it. He knew.

Glanson and the other war vet left the restaurant twenty minutes later. They walked in step to an older Honda Civic. The new guy drove. They got back on University and hit the nearest freeway entrance. LaDon followed at a distance, all the time wondering what dispensary they were going to hit next. See, he knew by the way these two walked they were up to something. A no good something. LaDon saw that look in people every day—no mistaking the dumbass on a person's face. Or in the way they moved.

And when the Honda took an exit into downtown—Market Street—LaDon did too, thought maybe the war vets wanted a night on the town. The Civic parked on Market. He pulled farther along the street, watched them in his rearview mirror. The men started in his direction; he cruised another hundred yards or so before he found a spot. LaDon pulled in, reached a hand out the window, and twisted his mirror to see the opposite side of the street. He hunched down in the driver's seat. A moment later, two dark figures sauntered into view along the sidewalk. They hugged the wall between the small shops and offices, all those dark windows below the lighted apartments above them. LaDon said, "They're doing something, that's for sure." He looked around for cops, but all he saw were bums laid out on the sidewalk, a taxi passing now and again. He spoke aloud to himself: "Well, shit then."

He sat back and watched. May as well see how it's done.

May as fuck well.

TWENTY-TWO

In the car, on the way to the rasta man's shop, Echo tried to convince Glanson to do a different shop. See, Echo followed Glanson all day and he knew the rasta shop's money was cut—he'd seen Glanson do a money pickup there. Why were they going back? Echo didn't understand. As he steered the Civic onto the freeway, he said, "Why are we going to do a place downtown? Isn't that asking for trouble? You know how many cops are—"

"It'll be quick, buddy. And then we'll head somewhere else."

"Two joints in one night? That's fucking ridiculous, man. I fucking—"

"It's smart is what it is."

"How is that smart?" Echo noticed Glanson was agitated when they met in the restaurant. He kept bouncing one knee up and down, clinching his jaw. His knee bounced so hard now that the Civic shook with it at sixty miles per hour. "Hey, man, what the fuck is up with you tonight? I mean, you're not cool like the other night."

Glanson said, "Exit Market Street, hang a left."

"Glanson," Echo said, "If I'm in this with you, man, you got to—"

"Fucking bitch."

"What?"

"I can't believe that fucking bitch. I can't fucking believe it."

"Tell me you aren't upset over a girl. Lots of women in the world, buddy. Let's not go and get shot over a girl. You hear me? I didn't skin my ass in Eye-Rack to get shitcanned over some girl." Echo looked over at Glanson's knee—it bounced up and down so fast it looked like three. "Man, are you fucking hearing me?"

Glanson nodded with the whole upper half of his body. "I went through the shit too, you motherfucker. And that bitch has no fucking idea. No fucking clue about what I am. Treat me like a fucking piece of shit? I don't think so…"

"Glanson! Don't get stupid-angry over a woman!" Echo took the Market Street exit with a violent jerk. He turned left and the tires squealed.

"Fine, motherfucker. You don't want to get shot over a woman? Tell me, what the fuck would you get shot over? What do you want to die for?"

Echo didn't have to think about it. "Money," he said.

"That's good. Park your ass right there," Glanson said pointing to a spot on the street's north side. "Make sure you're ready to do what you did the other night."

Darkness. Scattered lights on the opposite side of the street. Light traffic, but plenty of people to see them clinging to the building. Echo didn't like how this job felt to him. He had that I'm-gonna-get-fucked feeling. He whispered in Glanson's ear, "You sure about this, man? What are we doing exposed like this?"

No answer. Glanson moved beneath a streetlight, revealed his pistol.

Echo thought: Fuck me, man.

Both men lowered black ski masks over their faces.

Echo watched Glanson approach a door with a small window next to it. He couldn't see the shop's name as close as he was to the building, but he did see rasta beads draped across the window, knew it must be the dispensary. As Echo reached the window, Glanson lifted a foot and slammed it into the door. The door burst inward, and the sound of glass shattering reached the street. Glanson moved into the office and Echo followed—he raised his own pistol.

The rasta man's voice hit them as they entered: "The fuck is this?" He loomed in a doorway beyond a shattered glass display case—the door crashed through it after Glanson's blow.

The rasta had something in his hand.

Glanson, well in front of Echo, hesitated and didn't take a shot—he paid for it with blood.

Echo saw the shotgun come up to meet them and he backed out of the doorway, spun onto the sidewalk. The blast rang in his ears. Before Echo returned fire, Glanson hobbled out into the night. He didn't have his pistol anymore and one side of his face was a mix of black thread and skin. Blood poured across his chest, down to his crotch.

He stumbled twice, turned toward Echo.

Glanson said, "Ith hurths."

"I'll fucking bet," Echo said and started walking fast along the sidewalk, back toward the Civic.

He sensed Glanson following and turned to look. The big rasta with flapping dreads came out onto the sidewalk. "Fuck you, motherfuckers!"

The shotgun roared again and Glanson got hit. He lurched, fell, started crawling.

Echo saw the rasta start to reload. Fuck me, man. He ran back to Glanson, tugged, got him on his feet. Together, they jogged to the next corner, somehow got into the Civic and Echo started the engine. He maneuvered out of their spot, swung the Civic in a tight U-turn.

"One-way threet," Glanson said.

Echo didn't respond; he floored it and made the next right. Two cars whipped past them, all horns and squealing brakes. He heard the shotgun once more before he accelerated onto the freeway. He looked over at Glanson in the passenger seat and said, "You almost got me killed."

"I'm fucked up, man. I'm bleeding."

"Yeah," Echo said. He changed lanes, careful to stay at the speed limit. "And it doesn't look like it's going to stop."

TWENTY-THREE

LaDon saw the blast before the sound reached him. He sat up in his seat, watched as the two men darted out of the office, Jessie's guy stumbling and falling, trying to right himself.

They started moving down the sidewalk and a big man with dreadlocks ran out of the office, planted his feet, and fired a shotgun at them. Again, he hit Jessie's guy and the man went down, started to crawl. It surprised LaDon when the man's partner went back and helped him up—they managed to outrun the rasta's reload and hop back into the Civic.

LaDon watched in the rearview mirror as the Civic reversed, pulled forward, flipped a bitch on the one-way street. Brakes squealed and horns blew as the Civic accelerated, made a turn, and disappeared from LaDon's view. Well, that shit sure did not go as planned. The rasta shook his head and ran back into the office.

LaDon started the Cutlass, pulled casually into light evening traffic. He reached over and flipped on the radio. He pointed himself toward The Zip Zap Bar.

Now that the show was over, LaDon wanted a drink to think things through.

TWENTY-FOUR

"Take me to a hothpital, buddy. Pleath." Glanson's one good eye watched Echo from the passenger seat. His blood soaked the car; it was on the window, the door, the center console, pooling on the seat and on the floorboard.

Echo sat there shaking his head. They were back in Mid-City, a dark residential street Echo turned onto when he couldn't think of what to do. "I can't, buddy. You know I can't."

Glanson was silent for a few minutes.

Echo watched the street, ready to take off if somebody approached.

Glanson said, "C'mon. Take me to a hothpital."

"Can't do that, buddy."

"I juth wanted to thcare him," Glanson said. He coughed blood.

"You saying you weren't going to rob that joint?"

"To get more bithness. Thath why…"

Jesus. Echo did not believe that, but there it was. Fuck.

"Do me a favor. Can you—"

"I am not taking your ass to a hospital."

"No. No." Glanson coughed hard. Drops of blood

flew from his mouth, landed on the dashboard and windshield. "My girl...Tell her what happened."

"You want me to tell your girl that you got killed trying to drum up business? That's so fucking romantic of you. You're such a fucking—"

"Here. Here." Glanson shoved a shaking hand into his pocket, came out with his cell phone. "Her athress is in there. Jetthie Jethup. Pleathe, man. Pleathe."

Echo shook his head. He thought about what to do. I can leave the car here, walk away and act like it's all good. No, the car's registered to me. What then? Burn it? He had a spare gas can in the trunk, a lighter in his pocket. Light it up, declare it stolen? No—that's no good. Go back to your apartment. Act like nothing happened. When the cops call, you say an old war buddy borrowed your car, a man named Abbicus Glanson. Did you know him well? Well enough, shit. I did some war with the man. And the next thing he'd hear: We have some bad news for you, Mr. Echo. That's it, that's what I'll do. I'll burn the car, go home, and play stupid. The money in the trunk—I need to get that before I leave. Echo looked at Glanson and sighed. "I don't know why you went in like that, buddy. You and me went through some shit way back when, and you were always crazy. Nuts. Fucking nuts. But not stupid. And I swear, man. Fuck. You didn't have to..."

No use talking to a dead man.

Echo looked away from the body and unlatched his seatbelt, left the keys in the ignition. He thought for a second more before taking the cell phone from Glanson's lifeless hand.

But he did it.

Then he stepped out into the night.

THE THREE

TWENTY-FIVE

Jessie didn't like it—how things went down with Abbie. And she had a funny feeling the following Monday when the white Econoline van parked out front of the dispensary. The driver climbed out—the burly boss man with the shaved head—and Abbie was nowhere to be seen. Fuck. Jessie watched Abel jog across the street, one hand pressed to the gun on his hip, and push in through the front door. She watched on the closed-circuit as he pressed the intercom in the waiting room. She buzzed him in and, once inside, he wiped sweat off his head, nodded at her.

"I'm here for the day's pick up," he said walking toward her desk.

"Where's Abbie?"

Abel looked out the window, shrugged. He had a vacant look in his eyes.

"He's too chicken-shit to pick up my money?"

"Lady, I don't know what you're thinking, calling a war veteran chicken-shit." Abel grunted and blew air through his lips. "Glanson was about the farthest thing from chicken-shit."

The way he said it put a hole in Jessie's stomach. So big you could drop a Mack truck through it.

"You know he was a decorated soldier?" Abel leaned on the desk with two fists. "But you don't give no shits about that, huh? I guess you just go on walking around, buying new underwear and drinking Diet Coke. Fucking watch another Hot Wives of Orange County or whatever."

Jessie cleared her throat. "I know he was in the service."

"Man was a war hero. Fuck the service...Leave a man out here to scrounge for himself."

Jessie didn't know what to say. Abel kept those vacant gray eyes on her and she felt like shivering. She wished LaDon was in the office, but he said he needed to see a bartender about their money. And could she run the place without him for the morning? Yeah. But I'd kind of really like to get this weirdo out of here. Jessie almost laughed thinking about it: take my money and leave, please. Like she was getting stuck up herself.

Abel said, "It's a fucking shame."

"What?" That hole in Jessie's stomach was bigger, a giant fucking mouth you could fly a 747 into, never see the thing come back out.

"What?"

"That's what I said, what?"

Abel crossed his arms, stood over the desk like a bald white statue. "Glanson's dead. Burned up a couple miles from here. As the crow flies."

Jessie's jaw unhinged without her permission. She didn't blink. She was suddenly aware—in great detail—of the marijuana scents surrounding her. Pink Cush, Neon Mirage, Wild Ass Wax...a whole bunch of others. Sounds, too, came at her like images: She heard a trash truck's brakes squeal, a chopper humming over the city, her own breathing hot in her ears. This happened to her once before when she got news about her sister's death. She was sitting in an ugly diner off 247, looking out the window at tumbleweeds and mountains. Fucking sheriff's deputy talking to her like she was a child. And her own words coming out: How? Who? Why? He said, a car accident and we don't know and we never know. It just was, you know?

Jessie heard herself say, "Burned up?"

"An old buddy's car. Glanson burned up in it. On a fucking city street, if you believe that. Not one fucking asshole tried to save the man."

"Was it a car accident?"

"You can call it that, but the cops say it was on purpose."

Jessie gulped. "You're saying he was murdered?"

"Look, I got other pickups today, okay? I can't stand here and play twenty fucking questions. What I learned in the war, the only thing I learned, is that being dead sucks but you don't come back from it. Was he murdered? Maybe? Is he coming back from it? Not in this fucking life, lady. I'll have another man hired in the next couple weeks. It's just that I have to do a round of background checks and have training sessions and—"

"Abbie's gone," Jessie said.

Abel nodded. "Now you're getting it."

"Dead."

"That's the word for it."

"Jesus Christ," Jessie said.

"If you believe in the dude, sure. I'm not too sure if Glanson did. He struck me as a not-giving-a-fuck kind of dude, but I could be wrong. You never know who's been saved."

Jessie leaned over and lifted a gray duffel bag from the floor. "Here's the money."

Abel grabbed the handles, let the bag swing to his side. His other hand went to the pistol on his hip. "Thanks for your business, lady. Sorry for the shift in personnel. I'll have another man on it in a few weeks."

Jessie nodded, but the hole inside her was bigger than the world.

TWENTY-SIX

LaDon took his regular seat at The Zip Zap Bar, sat watching Zim the bartender pour a gin and soda for a skinny white dude in cutoff Levi shorts. When Zim came over and popped a beer for him, LaDon said, "What kind of trash is coming in here now?"

"Kind that pays with crushed dollar bills, man. Kind that got the shakes."

"Shit," LaDon said watching the white guy lift the shaking glass to his lips. "And I thought I drank too damn much."

"You do."

"I ain't shaking, am I?"

"Not yet, but don't think you won't get the hang of it."

LaDon smirked, put the cold beer bottle to his cheek. "You got us some deposit numbers?"

"Give me a minute."

Zim crossed through the bar and turned left down a dim hallway. While LaDon waited, he spun on his stool and watched a sports talk show on an old school TV sitting above the pool tables. The sound was muted and it was just chubby dudes in fancy ties moving their lips. LaDon couldn't remember the last time he sat down and watched an entire sporting event. Maybe a boxing match a few months back, and that because he had some money on it.

That's right, LaDon remembered he lost a hundred bucks on a bantamweight out of Jacksonville. Fucking Floridians. They didn't have shit on SoCal fighters. Nobody did but the Mexicans, you asked LaDon about it. He turned around and Zim was pouring more gin into the white guy's glass, the guy bouncing on his skinny legs and nodding like a little kid. Zim finished and walked over to LaDon, slid a printed sheet of paper across the bar.

LaDon looked at the sheet and saw a series of deposits ranging from four hundred dollars to two thousand dollars. The deposits were spread across three banks, all Bahamian. "These here the account numbers?"

"That's right. All you need to do is call down there and get your access set up. We made the accounts just like you said, that funny password and authentication." Zim leaned on the bar and sniffed hard through a plugged nostril. "And I took my fee like we agreed."

"How'd you get the money down there, Zim?" LaDon eyeballed the bartender.

"Tricks of the trade, baby. I have a whole list of sophisticated clientele. Lots of dudes I know need to get their money into banks. I look at it like a trade secret, you know? I tell you how I do it and what you got to pay me for?"

"I don't know if I'd call drug dealers sophisticated," LaDon said.

"You think you're any better?"

"I work security for a dispensary—weed's fucking legal."

"Whatever, man. You ain't got a city permit, you

ain't paying taxes, and you sure as shit ain't playing it by the book. You might be a bigger crook than a crack dealer." Zim raised his eyebrows and waited for LaDon's comeback to that.

LaDon grunted, finished his beer. "And you're saying I can access this money when I want it?"

"Long as you set it up with the banks. They're good at this kind of thing."

LaDon stared at the sheet of paper for a minute longer. He shrugged and said, "Fuck it. Better than all our money sitting in a safe, waiting to get took. I never thought I'd have a too-much-money problem, but you never know where life will take you."

"No such thing as a too-much-money problem. Me and you, we can solve this together."

LaDon laughed. "I just fucking bet. Let me guess... for a fee?"

"You got it, baby."

LaDon climbed off the stool and picked up a gray duffel bag beside him. He set it on the bar.

Zim grabbed the bag and lifted it with a slight exhalation of breath. He dropped the bag and grinned. "We looking at more?"

"Fifty g's," LaDon said. "Can you do that?"

"It's going to be a while, but I can do it. Yeah, I can do it."

LaDon finished his beer. "How much I owe you?"

"I'm pleased to buy you a drink," Zim said in his best Hollywood barman interpretation.

"Good," LaDon said, "and I ain't tipping your ass."

As LaDon walked out of the bar, he nodded at the jumpy white guy. The glass in his hand kept shaking. LaDon wondered if it was ever going to stop.

* * *

The Cutlass rolled easy down University. Bright sunlight reflected off the golden hood. LaDon pulled aviator sunglasses over his big eyes and turned up James Brown on the radio. They got some money in the bank. All they had to do was keep getting it in the bank. After seeing the security man get shot, LaDon wanted all of his and Jessie's money back—the trick was how to do it. You can't ask for it all at once, otherwise things look weird. Yeah, it's our money, but it'd look funny to ask for it. To demand it. This got LaDon thinking about ripping off M&J Security.

He hooked a left onto Forty-fourth, cruised through a cramped neighborhood with cars parked end-to-end on each side of the street. What I can do, LaDon told himself, is follow the white van, find out where they keep the money. LaDon knew it was a secure location, but how secure?

You need to find out, LaDon.

And you might need some dynamite. Wait, you think they're using a safe? No, LaDon saw Glanson and the other one, Abel, were too fucking arrogant for that. Like how Glanson tried to rip off the rasta, wandering in off the street like he's buying a forty or something. Fucking moron. LaDon remembered the shotgun blast and Glanson falling, his buddy coming back to help him. That's what the streets will give you if you're too fucking stupid.

LaDon made a left onto El Cajon, cruised over the freeway toward the dispensary. Three city buses were lined up at the transit station, taillights flashing. A man on a beach cruiser weaved across three lanes, his hairy arms jutting out from beneath a frumpy Lakers jersey.

Don't be stupid, LaDon. Get your money. He did some math in his head: Take our money and multiply that by, say, ten-twelve other dispensaries. What's that give you? Average it at one hundred g's a week each and that's…a million bucks the security guys take in a week? Was that right? Three, four million a month? No—can't be that much.

LaDon doubted it for a second, but then he thought: that's got to be right. Or close.

And maybe it's more.

Fuck it. You know what? Get everybody's money, LaDon. Come across money like that and LaDon planned to keep Zim in business from now until eternity.

The radio station moved into some Sly Stone. LaDon stopped at the next red light, bobbed his head slightly to the funk coming out of the speakers. Man, it was a nice day. And LaDon felt good. No, LaDon felt fucking stellar.

TWENTY-SEVEN

Echo started in on the whiskey at seven in the morning. Since last week, when he left Glanson to burn up in his shitty Civic, Echo couldn't function without alcohol running through his veins. A lot of fucking alcohol. Not so much that Glanson was dead—crazy motherfucking Glanson—but that Echo was nervous about the cops. They'd appeared at the apartment door twice yesterday, a different patrol cop each time. Each guy knocking and shouting through the door. But Echo didn't answer. He sat on the dirty floor next to the refrigerator and sipped his whiskey. Eventually, both cops left. Not like it was a bank robbery they were investigating. Hell, they probably thought Glanson stole the fucking Civic. What was Echo afraid of?

He just didn't like cops. Hated the fuckers. Like he hated his drill sergeant and the hajjis.

So many motherfuckers to hate in this world.

And what about this chick Glanson made Echo promise to see?

He sat at his kitchen table drinking the whiskey and thinking about the woman. Echo didn't like knocking on the woman's door, taking the risk that a neighbor might see him as a house guest. And after the lady's boyfriend gets turned to barbecue? Not the best look. So, he needed to play it cool, sneak into her place and surprise her.

How are you? I'm one of Glanson's old war buddies.

How'd he die?

Well, it's not too long a story...

Echo figured he didn't owe Glanson a fucking thing, that he could ditch the guy's cell phone and never see the woman. Nobody would know a damn thing about it.

I'd know.

Me.

That got to Echo, got him thinking—still, like a soldier—that he needed to honor the dead man's final wishes.

Another voice in his head he wished would shut the fuck up. For once. Forever.

After the whiskey, he tried drowning the voice out with Megadeth blasting in his headphones, swirling guitar solos and heavy thumps pounding his brain. Still there. Fuck. It whispered to him about Glanson rushing into buildings and clearing spaces ahead of Echo. It told a story about Glanson shooting a teenager with an RPG before Echo's Humvee got blown to metal bits.

Fuck. Fuck. Fuck.

You don't need to see the woman. Glanson won't know the difference. And another voice gasped, said again that Echo would know the difference. How you think it'll be to live with yourself if you don't talk to the woman? Miserable? Miserable. Fucking-A, right.

Now that he was out of the service, Echo didn't go for this honorable brother bullshit. But Glanson—as crazy as the fucker was—saved Echo's life. Saved a lot of other American lives too. Goddamn right. Fucking-A, right. He threw his headphones across the apartment, winced as they slammed into a wall. He found a bottle of vodka in the freezer. That went down cold, sat in his belly like mercury. At the table, he measured the whiskey and vodka against each other. Out of whiskey, go ahead with the vodka. He threw the whiskey bottle at the refrigerator. It didn't shatter on impact, but instead when it hit the tile floor. Clean that up later. Tomorrow.

Like everything else in his fucking life.

Alright. Alright. Echo downed the rest of the vodka in the bottle. Sat there while his chest and throat burned. He walked into the bedroom and stared at the two stacks of cash in the center of the bed. Not enough money to do anything with, not really. He opened a dresser drawer and got his gun. Still loaded. Should have plugged that rasta, the one with the shotgun. Maybe I still will. Could he do that instead of going to see the woman? No—not the same thing. Not what Glanson wanted. He shoved the gun into his waistband, chose a new Hawaiian shirt, this one with toucans flying everywhere across it. Echo wasn't sure toucans lived in Hawaii. Fuck it. Like everything else.

Except for seeing the woman. Had to do that. Had to go through with it.

Before he left the apartment, Echo pried aside the blankets duct taped to the windows and peeked outside. He didn't see any cops. Bunch of cars parked beneath still palm trees.

He took inventory of the cars and, a half block away, he saw a matte black Honda Civic a year or two older than his own model. One thing Echo knew about those cars, they were easy to steal. Early morning and bright outside, but hardly anybody on the street.

Time for Echo to hitch a ride.

TWENTY-EIGHT

When Jessie heard the bump of bass around the corner, she started locking up the dispensary. No customers right that minute and—after clamping the safe and twisting the locks on her storage shelves—she moved through the waiting room, turned for a moment to look up at the security camera. She knew that look was recorded on the hard drive in her office. She wanted to run back through the footage, see Glanson wandering in the last time he picked up her money, his wispy hair waving as he loped through the camera shot and got buzzed in. Damn—Abbie was dead.

She didn't believe it.

By the time Jessie got outside, LaDon's gold Cutlass was slowing to a stop beside the curb. The bass still bumped in LaDon's trunk. He saw her moving toward him and the music died as he lowered the volume. LaDon leaned over and rolled down the Cutlass's passenger side window.

Jessie leaned into the car, though she might look like a prostitute to a passing patrol cop. LaDon, the big black man sitting in the car, was maybe her man, her pimp. Jessie said, "You and me need to talk about something. Let's go and get some lunch."

"What is it?"

"A private thing," Jessie said.

"Get in, I guess."

Jessie unlatched the door and slid into the air freshened atmosphere of the Cutlass. Easy to see LaDon took care of the car; the dashboard glowed like it was elixered with Armor-All, and the seats—despite the car's age—felt new and plush. "Something happened," she said.

LaDon, still sitting with one hand casual atop the steering wheel, turned his big intelligent eyes on her. "You okay, Jessie?"

"Abbie—" She stopped herself. "Glanson, he's dead."

With his same disinterested expression, LaDon said, "You talking the security man? Your Mr. Romeo? He got put down?"

Jessie felt like screaming at him. What an asshole to say it like that. "Yeah," she said all sarcastic, "my fiancé. Turns out, he got himself killed."

LaDon looked confused. After thinking her statement through, he said, "I'm sorry, Jess. Didn't mean to sound like a dick—I got something on my mind."

"Me too. Like how the fuck do we get our money—"

"I told you I'm working on that." LaDon pulled his eyes off her and let them wander out the windshield, settle on the front of a neighborhood liquor store. "I need more though. The first bit went through just fine."

Jessie was surprised. She knew LaDon knew people, but she doubted he'd be the one to figure out the money part. "We got it back?"

"It's on vacation down in the Bahamas, but we can have it whenever we want."

"Thank God," Jessie said.

"And thank my connect with the money know-how,

may peace be upon him." LaDon sniffed hard and ran a hand along his bald head. "What happened to your crush?"

"He got burned up in a car, a few miles east." Jessie stared out the window now, but she felt LaDon's eyes burn into her face. "Dead as a dog biscuit. Cops said he might have been..."

"Murdered?"

"Yeah," Jessie said. And with more verve, "Yes. Murdered." She didn't look, but she knew LaDon must be shaking his head. "You were right about it being a bad idea." She got defensive then, and she added, "About the money service, I mean."

"We need to get our money the fuck back with us. And we need to do it ASAP."

"I'm with you on that, LaDon."

"And we need to keep this business—and I'm talking the whole damn business—between us two, okay? No more subcontracting or whatever the fuck."

"We didn't know what to do with the money, how to handle it. And I—"

"You did the best you could. Now, we got another way. It's slow, but we can do more and more, especially the more we get. There's the problem of the fee, but..."

"We pay M&J two grand a month."

"We gonna save that money," LaDon said.

Jessie nodded. "Use it to invest in ourselves." They sat there in the Cutlass for a long while, neither of them speaking. Jessie didn't know what to say. With Abbie gone, Jessie felt that LaDon was the only man she had in her world. Matter of fact, it was just the two of them against the world. Wasn't that the song? Yes, it was. And she could do worse than LaDon. Way the fuck worse. And reverse it, okay? She sure as shit couldn't do much better. She looked over at LaDon and said, "You're sitting there real quiet. What is it?"

He rubbed a big hand along a chubby cheek and smirked. "How many shops you think they pick up from? How much money you think they got?"

"I don't know. What's that got to do with us?"

"Nothing, except they got more money than us."

"It's not theirs."

"Right," LaDon said, "they're just holding it."

"Yeah. Yes."

"Like a bank."

"It's just like a bank," Jessie said.

"Except it ain't like a bank. It's not a damn sight close to a bank." He wiggled his finger at the liquor store. "I don't see no brick-and-mortar location, you can run inside and yank the manager's balls if you got a complaint. You see that?"

"LaDon, we need somewhere to stash the money—you fucking know that."

He nodded slowly and looked at her, dangled his large right arm over the bench seat. "Jessie, let me ask you: you ever thought what to do with a million dollars?"

She shook her head.

"I want you to think about it."

"Why?"

"Because when we get that M&J money, and we're gonna get it, you need to have a plan for it."

"I still don't know what you're saying."

"I'm saying we gonna get our motherfucking money back. And we gonna get everyone else's along with it. You can call that ransom money."

Jessie gulped. The hole in her stomach was bigger

than when she heard Abbie was dead. She wondered, who are all these fucking men in my life?

"You mind we get some Mexican food?" LaDon swung the Cutlass east and accelerated through a yellow light. He expected Jessie to come up with some shitty vegan joint they could visit and he was surprised when she didn't.

"Whatever." She stared out the window with a listless look on her face.

LaDon shrugged, took them past a bunch of carnicerias, two or three different tortilla shops. They passed a sidewalk florist and a bunch of little kids getting out of elementary school in their navy blue uniforms and collared white shirts. He thought: Training motherfuckers to fall in line right from the start. LaDon ran another yellow light and hooked a right onto 42nd. He cruised slowly until he saw the small sign for Zeta's, a Mexican joint between a smog check station and body shop. LaDon stopped, made an illegal u-turn, and parked right out front of the place—in fact, he parked behind a fast-looking black Impala.

My old pal Moonie Sykes, LaDon told himself, is wrong as hell in the head.

But the man is always right when it comes to shit like this.

Once inside, LaDon spotted Eddie and the white girl—Ginny, right?—huddled next to each other in a back booth. The girl plucked at a basket of tortilla chips, bit them like she didn't want to mess up her black lipstick. Eddie stared out the window, one hand brushing absently across Ginny's neck. Neither of them saw

LaDon saunter in with Jessie at his side.

Jessie and LaDon moved to the front counter and read the menu.

Jessie grunted and said, "This place a favorite of yours?"

"It's okay…"

"Wow, aren't we living the high life?"

LaDon shrugged. He liked the smell of carnitas and Mexican beer. Those scents made his stomach growl—it didn't matter where he found the smell. Could be a little counter down in Tijuana or a greasy joint up here in Mid-City. All that mattered to LaDon was the meat and salsa. He figured Zeta's for authentic Mexican, especially given the name.

But before his lunch, LaDon needed to take care of Eddie.

Jessie ordered a veggie burrito and glared at LaDon with those nice green eyes, dared him to make fun of her.

He said, "I'll take the carne asada burrito and three tacos al pastor." He paid with a credit card. "Don't worry, Jess, I'm the money man."

"And I got the goods," she said.

They sat in a booth along the front windows. LaDon sat on the edge of the bench and crossed his arms, watched Eddie rub the white girl's slim neck. Jessie punched at her cell phone screen. It didn't take long for the white girl to see LaDon and whisper something into her pimp's ear.

LaDon smiled when she did that. A second later he was across the little shop staring down at Eddie. "You and me have some business together," he said.

"The fuck we do." Eddie bit the corner of his upper

lip, revealed one yellow dog tooth.

"Get on up," LaDon said. "We gonna make this quick."

Eddie's eyes got angry and he lifted his chin. "I still got that piece if you want to—"

LaDon's bulk smothered the booth and the two humans inside it. He cut Eddie off with a two-handed grip on his head, LaDon's big hands mashing each side of Eddie's face together. He lifted the skinny pimp out of his seat and over Ginny—the slim greaser kicked hard at the table and overturned the basket of tortilla chips— and set the man down with a violent shove that put him on his ass. Eddie scrambled to his feet and, at the same time, clutched at his waistband. But LaDon was on him like pepper on a steak—he pulled a bulky black pistol from Eddie's shaking left hand, the same gun Eddie pointed at LaDon a few nights prior.

LaDon said, "See if you can scare me without a torch."

Eddie shrank back against a bank of gumball machines and put his hands in front of his face.

In the booth, Ginny stared straight ahead. Her cheeks rippled with tension.

LaDon nodded at the emergency exit. Eddie walked ahead, pushed open the door. He tried to run as soon as his feet hit pavement but an old playground trick got the best of him. LaDon swung his size nineteen right foot forward and connected with one of Eddie's heels. The pimp's feet smacked together and he tumbled end over end, came up on his knees with a bloody nose and his own black pistol in his face.

LaDon smiled down at him and said, "How's this feel, you grimy motherfucker?"

"Like an excuse to kill you."

"You must be some kind of stupid." LaDon used the pistol to plant a blow between Eddie's shoulder and ear. A short sound like a dog vomiting came from the pimp's throat. He toppled onto his side and folded into the fetal position. LaDon bent over him and spit in his face. "Makes me sick, seeing a grease ball like you walking a girl around like she's a dog."

"A bitch is a bitch," Eddie said.

"Oh, man." LaDon stood and shoved the pistol into his waistband. He adjusted his collared shirt and sighed. After looking hard at Eddie once more, he reared back that size nineteen and brought it down—it made a crunching sound.

"You got somewhere to go?" LaDon dangled the Impala keys in front of Ginny. Like he was hypnotizing her.

"What happened to Eddie?"

"He's taking a nap. He'll be fine…In a couple weeks."

"I wanted to live in California," Ginny said. "I like the beach."

"Maybe you should try Florida."

She reached out and wrapped her fingers around the keys.

LaDon said, "Open your purse."

Ginny unlatched her bag, a purple thing with tassels, and LaDon dropped Eddie's gun into it.

When LaDon got back to the booth, Jessie was half-way through her veggie burrito and one of the tacos was missing. "You ate one of my tacos?"

Jessie grinned. "It looked too good."

Ginny passed behind them as she left Zeta's. LaDon

watched her unlock the Impala, climb in, and start it. He bit into his burrito, chewed, swallowed. "Damn, that's good."

The Impala squealed into traffic, turned the corner.

Jessie said, "What was that about?"

"Humanitarian work," LaDon said. "It's a hobby of mine."

TWENTY-NINE

Echo did lunch at a strip club down off Rosecrans, place called The Lady Shoppe. Fourteen bucks for a floppy cheeseburger and potato salad. He drained sixty bucks on lap dances from a skinny chick with a wedding ring tan on her finger. He thought how it wasn't a woman he wanted, but more money. Enough to take him down to South America. Enough to never come back. Echo considered himself a patriot but it was always better to be American somewhere else—he learned that on R&R while he was in the service.

The married chick slapped her ass with both hands and wiggled it in Echo's face. He bent down and kissed her crack. The song ended—some EDM shit—and Echo handed the stripper another twenty. She blew a kiss and let him be. A second later the cocktail waitress dropped off another bottle of beer and Echo put it to his lips. Yeah, he'd come to a decision about this thing with Glanson, this promise to a dead man. Echo was going to honor his word but he needed to be good and drunk. Well, drunker than the past few days. He looked over his shoulder for the cocktail waitress, held a finger aloft to signal a third shot of Jim Beam.

When he turned around Echo was face-to-face with a bearded man in a Knicks jersey. The man wore baggy black pants and a backwards baseball cap. His beard was full but well trimmed. Built lean—Echo took him for a GI right from the start. He nodded at the beard and said, "Have a beer with me, soldier."

"Don't mind if I do." Beard reached out a hand and they shook. "Call me Buzz."

"I'm Echo. When you get back, Buzz?"

"About two weeks ago." He glanced around the club, near empty this early in the afternoon, and settled his gaze on a plump looker doing a handstand on the stage. "Everywhere you go, you see some shit. I tell you, I'm surprised every day."

"First time in a gentleman's club?" Echo caught the cocktail waitress's eye again, signaled for an extra shot of Beam. "You look old enough."

"Just turned twenty-one, sir. We got one of these places back home but I never went."

"Where's home?"

"New Mexico."

"Beautiful country," Echo said. He watched Buzz for a response but the young soldier kept his eyes on the stripper. He made no expression as she cartwheeled onto her back and thrust her hips at the ceiling. The music was pop country from some Texas pretty boy. "Look, Buzz—"

The cocktail waitress set two shot glasses in front of them and swirled into the darkness.

"Have one with me?"

Buzz nodded.

They clinked glasses and drank. Echo said, "To gunfire, baby."

"To gunfire and hell raining down from above," Buzz said. He set the glass down and settled back into his seat. The stripper made it to the pole and started to work her way up, spun clockwise and inverted toward the ceiling. "And to more of the same."

"Headed back then, huh?" Echo cringed at his own question.

Buzz shrugged. "I love war, sir."

Echo doubted that, but he nodded. "Goddamn, don't we all?"

"We're killing machines."

"Fucking-A, right." Echo felt the liquor in his joints. He smirked. "I got me a few hajjis—tell you what." He leaned forward in his chair, peered at Buzz while sucking down beer. "Three in one day, matter of fact."

Buzz nodded. "Good day, sir. That's a real good day."

"You can bet your ass." Echo felt like an old boy now, like his twenty-eight years on Earth made him a wise man. "You want, I can tell you how it went—"

"I killed twenty men in one day," Buzz said. "And three kids."

On stage, the stripper did the splits once more, somersaulted to her feet, and walked off stage. The music changed from country to hip-hop and the DJ summoned a new girl to the stage.

Echo gulped and drank more beer. "You a stone-cold killer then, my man." He said it with a warble in his voice, like he spoke across a guitar string.

"Mass killer," Buzz said. "Mass murderer, if you want to be accurate."

"Look, Buzz...kid. It's how it is, man. You don't need to—"

"Feel bad about it. I know. It's not my fault. I'm just doing my job. Hey, look, you know where I can pick up a girl for some fun? I got money. I got lots of money." Buzz stood and smoothed down his Knicks jersey, sat back down with a queer grin.

"How you get to be a Knicks fan in New Mexico?"

Buzz looked down at his jersey, adjusted his cap. "We only got one TV station on the satellite back home. Some station out of New York...Came in kind of clear, and there you have it."

Echo said, "There's a bouncer named Jimmy outside—he'll get you a companion for the evening. Or two, if that's what you want. Look, Buzz...Maybe you should think about seeing someone about how it was over there, what you got pushed into."

"You see the fucking shrink?"

Echo didn't answer that.

"See, sir, I just need a good fuck and a good drunk. That's about all there is to it."

The cocktail waitress reappeared and said, "You need anything else?"

Echo hesitated but said, "Two more shots. And whatever else this guy wants. Do me a favor, have Jimmy swing by on his break."

The waitress nodded and pranced off to the bar. A Latina girl with a nice ass was on stage and Buzz squinted at her, started to nod his head to the music. The strip club had started to fill up; Echo noticed guys in work pants and boots, a few suits wandering toward the bar, everybody finding tables by the stage.

He watched Buzz for a moment longer, but decided he felt better watching the girls.

What I'll do is I'll talk to Jimmy and get the young buck set up with a girl, Echo thought. After that, I'll head out to see Glanson's lady. And I'll come clean about the whole thing.

That was Echo's mission: Come clean.

THIRTY

They did ten grand that afternoon. Jessie celebrated by drinking sangria on the patio at a nearby tapas place. Truth was, Jessie never imagined she'd pull in that much money at once. Not selling homegrown herb. She sipped sangria (red) and thought about all the marijuana money floating out there in the city. And what LaDon was saying, how M&J Security had a whole bunch of it just sitting there. For the taking. She watched a few punk kids skateboard past on the sidewalk. One of them flipped off a teenager sitting at the bus stop across the street. The teen returned the favor and Jessie heard a volley of curse words fading down the avenue.

She dabbed at a half-eaten skillet of paella, thought how she'd never been anywhere in her life. Not really, anyhow. She'd been to Mexico. To Tijuana and Calexico. Once all the way down to San Felipe to camp out and drink on the beach. Beyond those places—the American Southwest. And sure, Texas was a big place. A country all its fucking own. But Jessie wanted to see the Eiffel Tower, eat pho on a neon-lit street corner, sleep on a sailboat. Sleep on a sailboat? The fuck was that? Jessie laughed to herself and an older couple glanced at her, looked away.

She pounded more sangria, poured a new glass from the pitcher on her table. It was still warm outside, the sun sinking below the horizon only minutes before she got there. She wiped sweat from her head and arms, tried to tell herself that ten grand a day—more sometimes— was plenty of money for a woman her age. But something inside her wouldn't agree.

She drank more and thought: Fuck it, why not a hell of a lot more money?

Why not, Jessie? And why not you, Jessie?

When her pitcher ran dry, Jessie walked out onto the avenue. She passed a corner store, a shoe repair shop (really, shoe repair?), and one of those immigration offices where they made you a passport and a driver's license. If we steal this money, she thought, will I need a new identity?

No, that's the beauty in it. This money isn't banked. And the records don't matter because the feds don't see herb as legal. It's just money out there in the wherever, waiting for her and LaDon to take it. LaDon to take it. Jessie didn't plan on doing a goddamn thing. She'd talk with LaDon. More if that's what he wanted, or needed. But she didn't plan on using her hands until she could spend the money. Abbie was gone, and now it was time for Jessie to get gone.

Maybe she'd move to South America, buy herself some land. Keep a small garden of personal product. But nothing official—after the murder in Mid-City and what happened to Abbie, Jessie wanted out. For good. She spotted a cab and waved it down, got into the back seat.

The driver was a Somali guy with manicured fingernails and a constant smile. Jessie gave him the address for her apartment and after they turned south onto Thirty-seventh said, "How long you been doing this? Driving a taxi, I mean."

"Seven years. Almost every night for seven years. Since I got here from my country."

Jessie leaned back in the seat. She felt good from the sangria, kind of loose and excited. Like she was headed to a party. "Why don't you do something else?"

The driver's eyes met Jessie's in the mirror. "In my country, I was an engineer. Oil and gas, you know? Here, it's like I don't exist. All these numbers in my head, mathematics. It's there for nothing. You want to know why I don't do anything else?" He swung a left onto her street, pulled to the curb outside her apartment building. "It's because I'm not living. What do you call it in between your heaven and here?"

"Purgatory?"

"Yes, purgatory. That's how it is for someone like me."

Jessie nodded, started digging in her purse for cash. "You know what? It's not just you. That's how I feel all the fucking time." She stopped and stared at him in the mirror. "Does that surprise you?"

He nodded slowly, looked off down the street full of cars and little kids playing touch football under the flickering streetlamps.

Jessie clenched a bill and brought it out—a ten. She glanced at the meter and saw she owed eight bucks. She reached over the seat and handed the driver the money. "Keep the rest."

"Thank you."

"Don't thank me. It's not enough to buy your ass out of purgatory." She spilled out of the cab and walked toward her apartment, that excited feeling giving way to the grogginess of a worn off buzz. She meant to be cele-brating, so why did she feel so shitty? As she reached her front door, she realized: it was Abbie. She felt bad about how she handled things. No—ashamed. That was it. She never treated a person like that before, but she was fuck-ing surprised. A thing that small? Okay, it wasn't how she treated him. But what she thought before she dis-covered...Some part of her thought—really fucking thought—she might fall in love with Glanson. And now he was dead. More than that, burned to death. Small dick and all.

She slipped her key into the lock, jiggled open the apartment door. Dark in the living room this late in the evening. She kept the shades drawn on the front window and the rear slider. Jessie dropped her purse, kicked off her flats. She pulled her blouse over her head and dropped it on the carpet. Unclasped her belt and slacks next. Wiggled out of both and stepped out of them. She ran her thumbs down each side of her g-string, brought the straps up along her hips. They snapped against her skin. She sighed and hoped she had a bottle of white in the fridge. But before she walked into the kitchen, Jessie heard a slurring voice behind her:

"It's nice to meet you too," Echo said. "Glanson, my war buddy, told me so much about you."

THIRTY-ONE

"Why don't you just take your ass to one of those casa de cambio places? Wire the money down to somebody in Mexico, have 'em send it right back your way?" Moonie munched on a large burrito now, stared past LaDon at two teenage girls walking by on the sidewalk.

The way to Moonie's heart was through his stomach—LaDon knew that for damn sure. And now he had the man outside a greasy taco shop near Thirtieth and El Cajon.

Moonie said, "Why you didn't get nothing?"

"I already ate Mexican today. Had a burrito and some tacos."

"You telling me a big motherfucker like you ain't hungry again?" Moonie chomped with his mouth open, gave LaDon a meat-filled smile. "Suit your motherfucking self."

"I already thought about those cash changing places," LaDon said. "Thing about it is, it's not efficient. Not the way I want it to be. Plus, it makes a whole bunch more paperwork. Shit people can track, trace back to me and Jessie."

"What I'm thinking then is you put it in some other trade."

"Like what?" LaDon popped a piece of spearmint gum into his mouth, chewed while he watched the junkie use that street genius brain of his.

"Drugs, for one. Get you a brick. Break it up. Sell that shit on the street."

"How's that help me, Moonie? I take one kind of drug money and put it into another drug. When I get it back, I got the same fucking problem: A bunch of money I ain't supposed to have. Plus, I got all the risk of selling crank. Hell, no."

"Girls then," Moonie said. He finished his burrito and licked the fingertips on his right hand. "Get in on the skin trade. That's good money and it accrues. That's like, an investment."

"What I'm saying, Moonie, is what the fuck do I do with the money?"

"Go on and buy what the fuck you need or want, LaDon. You trying for a 401(k)? Man, I look at you and I see black. But sometimes I wonder, when it rains am I gonna see the black run off and get a white country club motherfucker underneath it? You know what I'm saying?"

"Moonie, I'm trying to get this money in a bank so I can get on the move."

"Like, out of town?"

"Yeah, me and Jessie."

"Okay, I'm seeing it. I got you. Sounds to me like you need a real money man. Not this shifty mofo over at The Zip Zap Bar." Moonie shook a finger at LaDon. "Mark my words, one time this dude gonna come back and say your money got lost, picked up by customs."

"But it wasn't."

"That's right—a little cost of doing business charge."

LaDon shrugged. "It's the best I got right now."

Moonie smiled again and said, "I hold it for you."

"Fuck that. I'm just rapping with you, Moonie. I'll get it worked out."

"I hope you do, brother. You bring me out here for a sweet conversation, or you want something from me?" He dug a long fingernail into his teeth, pried at a stringy piece of meat. He dislodged it and sucked hard through pursed lips.

LaDon chewed his gum, looked around at the other customers. Two cooks from the Chinese joint across the street and a young couple with tattoos and body piercings. Nobody who gave a fuck. He said, "I want you to follow a guy for me. You still got that Toyota, the white one?"

"Shit, yeah I do. An eighty-three hatchback Corolla. About live in the motherfucker."

"I just want a record of what he does. Nothing else. I'm talking places and times, how and when he ends the day. Maybe, say, three-four days. I'll give you fifty a day, plus gas money."

Moonie straightened his lips. "Seventy-five, plus gas money."

"You keep them receipts," LaDon said.

Moonie's jaw dropped. "You gonna write this off, or what?"

"I want proof, if I'm paying your ass."

Moonie shook his head, chuckled. "Alright, LaDon."

"This ain't a thing but a watch job. You watch and write it down."

"Where I pick the guy up at?"

LaDon nodded, licked his bottom lip. "Run down to Mickey D's after we done here. Man does lunch over there, I heard."

"What if he ain't there?"

"You can wait outside our place tomorrow. He should swing by around three. White Econoline van, one of those long ones with the—"

"I know what it is."

LaDon scratched his chin and thought for a bit. Was it smart to bring Moonie in on this? No, but he needed to know Abel's movements over a few days, make sure he got to the storage unit and left it at the same times. He could pay Moonie off easy, and that made this work.

"What you going to do to the man?"

LaDon glared at Moonie. "I say I was gonna do anything to him?"

"No, but I'm guessing you got a reason to send me—"

"You stop guessing about shit," LaDon said. "Don't fuck it up and I'll throw down an extra hundo for the work. That make sense to you?"

"Jackpot, baby."

LaDon stood and slapped hands with Moonie, left him sitting there eating those vinegar-soaked carrots you can get at Mexican places. LaDon got into his Cutlass— parked behind the taco shop near a dumpster—and fired her up. He blew a bubble, popped it, spit the gum out the window and made an unprotected left onto El Cajon.

On the boulevard, LaDon kept one hand on the wheel, the other dangling outside the window. He thought he needed to run all this by Jessie, make sure she was okay with Moonie doing the surveillance on Abel. Not that she'd want something different, but La-Don wanted to be straight with her all the way through. Yeah, run it by her. Tonight, in fact. If they were in this, they better be in it together. Maybe now, after all this shit, Jessie might see him different.

Maybe she'd put that sweet little ass on LaDon's big bouncing knee.

THIRTY-TWO

"How drunk are you, on a scale of one to ten?" Jessie held one arm across her bare breasts, felt the guy's dirty brown eyes as they drank in her body.

"I'm at about eleven." He crossed one leg over the other. Decided that wasn't comfortable, set both feet flat on the shaggy carpet. "In case you want to know, my friends call me Echo."

Jessie shivered and said, "You mind if I put my clothes back on?"

"It's better for me if you don't." He cleared his throat, wiped a hand across his wet mouth.

Jessie switched arms across her boobs, ran her fingers through her hair. She felt dirty there with this guy looking at her. "I'm not sure what Abbie told you about me, but—"

"Abbie? That's cute. Super cute. Didn't know my buddy had a soft side like that."

"That's just what I called him."

Echo nodded, crossed his arms. He looked at ease on the couch. Very still and sure of himself. "So, you heard about what happened?" He sniffed hard, pinched the bridge of his nose.

To Jessie, the apartment felt cold and silent. She heard

the sound of water running through pipes below, a few sirens far out in the city. Not much else. She wanted to crawl into bed and pull the blankets over herself, forget about Abbie and this war buddy of his. She wanted to wrap herself in a new skin, forget about this old one being touched and prodded by Echo's eyeballs.

Echo didn't wait for her response. "Shame to go through a fucking war, make it all the way through that, come back home and burn up like a hot dog."

"What do you know about it?" Jessie dropped her arm and let her nipples glare at Echo. She walked over to her small dining table, pulled out one of the four chairs and sat. The apartment was small and combined the living and dining areas with the kitchen. Jessie crossed her legs, leaned back into the chair with one arm draped across the table. He wanted to see her tits? Fine, let him look. That's all he was going to get.

Echo leaned forward, put his elbows on his knees. He lifted his chin at her and smirked. In the deepening darkness, his mouth looked scratched on by charcoal. "Me and Glanson went through some shit. It don't feel right, him being dead."

Jessie nodded, bit the inside of her right cheek. "Me and him had a thing the other night. It didn't go well. I wish I had another shot at it, but..."

"What do you do, right?"

"Right."

"Thing is, Glanson told me to tell you something before he—"

"You were there?"

"I talked to him," Echo said as a knowing look crossed his face. Already, he put himself there. "That doesn't mean I was there. He called me before he—"

"Right," Jessie said. "He found time to call you, give you a message, send my address. And all before he got burned to hell in an—" She made air quotes "—accident that took his life."

Now Echo smiled. The only light in this cruel darkness. "He texted me, actually."

Jessie didn't believe that for a fucking nanosecond. "I'm sure," she said, the words coming out like a punch line in a joke. Some shitty joke.

"He wanted me to tell you, he got done by a dispensary owner. He was just trying to get some more business and, boom." Echo clapped his hands once for effect.

Jessie lifted her eyebrows. "Who did it?"

"Not me."

"Who the fuck killed Abbie?"

"Some rasta fuck downtown."

"Christ," Jessie said. Her thoughts went to all the marijuana plants in her bedroom, the harvested buds she had in a large plastic box. All of it just sitting there, waiting for some asshole to find out about it and come in here to...

"So," Echo said, "I'm guessing you have some money laying around here."

Jessie sighed.

Echo stood and removed a gun from beneath his shirt. It was a threatening black pistol, make and model unknown to Jessie. He waved it at her casually, almost as an afterthought. She didn't doubt that he was drunk, but he didn't move like he was drunk—that thought put fear in her heart. Made her see that he was a wild person, like someone she didn't often encounter.

"I'd like to leave here with some cash," Echo said. "I'm sure you understand."

"Let me make sense of this: You come here to tell me my guy is dead and now you want to rip me off? That's how you pay your condolences?"

"I was closer with Glanson than you ever would have got."

"How's that?"

"Brothers in arms," Echo said. He tapped his heart and pointed the gun at her. "Take me to the moola, sister."

Jessie stood and walked down the hall, conscious of her swinging hips and swaying naked breasts. Echo followed and Jessie still felt his dirty eyes on her, now taking in her slim backside and nice legs. She led him into the bedroom and kneeled beside the dresser, started to open a bottom drawer.

"Wait a second. You sit on the bed."

Jessie obeyed and sat on the bed, the sheets cool against her bare ass. She watched as Echo slid the drawer open, tossed her panties out onto the carpet.

He found a large manila envelope, peered inside it.

He nodded, straightened. The envelope got shoved into his waistband, covered by his shirt.

Jessie said, "There you have it."

"The way Glanson told it, you motherfuckers have more money than you know what to do with."

"He exaggerated."

Echo sighed. "I don't think so, Jessie." He stared at her for a long slow minute. "I'm only going to ask this one time, okay? Where's the rest of it—all the money you have?"

LaDon parked a few blocks from Jessie's apartment, all the closer parking spaces filled this late in the evening.

He locked the car, started walking east, and had a funny thought: maybe I should bring my shotgun. He hesitated, walked back to the car. Unlocked and opened the trunk.

The neighborhood was still and silent. LaDon looked out over the street packed with cars and shoddy apartment buildings. He wondered why it was so quiet this evening—it didn't seem normal to him. The air was warm and syrupy.

No way, he thought, I don't need a gun. What for?

He closed the trunk and locked the Cutlass again.

One block east, LaDon turned north on Jessie's block. The scent of BBQ meat hit him as he passed a duplex with cardboard over the front windows; LaDon saw two men out front with low brim baseball caps drinking beer and turning meat on a charcoal grill. He knew the tattoos on their necks and forearms—gang-related. LaDon lifted a hand in greeting. The men didn't wave back, but instead stared him down, watched as he sauntered past on the sidewalk.

He knew they kept watching him as he jogged across the street, took the broken cement path into Jessie's U-shaped apartment complex. He reached the staircase below Jessie's apartment and stopped. That odd feeling came at him again. He kept thinking he needed his gun.

But what for? Why the nerves, LaDon?

He looked over his shoulder, expected to see Steady Eddie the pimp coming after him. Maybe that was it? I'm spooked, LaDon thought. All this shit with Glanson getting shot by the rasta man and me beating the pimp into submission. This shit Moonie talked to me about over lunch. The money me and Jessie need to wash. It's got me nervous and stressed the fuck out—that's all it is.

And a gun ain't going to do shit about that.

He shook his head, looked back to the staircase, and started to climb the steps.

When he got halfway to the landing, LaDon heard a loud crash.

And then he heard a shout—a woman's voice.

Jessie—this hot bitch with tan tits and ass—didn't answer Echo the way he expected.

He didn't like that.

She said something like, "Go fuck yourself," but before she got it all out Echo had her by the hair. He threw her across the bed and the momentum carried her into the wall. Her left leg plunged through the sheetrock. Two large picture frames and a wall mirror came down, landed with a crash. She rolled and tugged her leg out of the drywall, white powder showering down onto her naked body. She got to her knees and started to scream.

Echo shut her up with a quick jab to the chin.

Now, she eye-fucked him while he propped her up on the bed—taking a healthy dose of free tits and ass in each hand—and leaned back against the dresser, his gun a prominent prop in his right hand. Echo said, "I told you not to fuck with me. God, Lee. I don't like a smart mouth on a woman. Fuck, I don't like a smart mouth on anybody. I mean, who does?"

Jessie ran a hand across her face, winced as she touched her chin.

"Hurts, huh?"

She pushed her tongue against a cheek and stared.

"Look, now," Echo held out his hands as if surprised by a referee's bad call. "I told you what I wanted and you didn't give it to me." He pointed the gun at her again. "I hate to kill a woman. I got a taste for killing men over in the Eye-Rack. But women? No, I never liked it—too goddamn easy. What's going to happen, no matter what, is I'm going to toss this place. I'll find the fucking money. All of it. Or most of it. You know that. The only question is how hurt you're going to be afterwards. Or how dead." He sniffed hard and lowered the gun, shrugged.

"I didn't know there were degrees of dead," Jessie said.

"There's that smart mouth again, but you're right," Echo said. "I guess it's only one variation of dead. You're either breathing or you're not. That's what the doctors say."

Jessie rubbed her forehead, seemed trapped in her pain. "The money's in the spare bedroom. I have a small safe, but I'll open it for you."

They were getting somewhere. "You go on and do that."

He followed her out of the bedroom and into the hallway, felt a tingle in his lower stomach as he thought about taking a piece of her perfect little ass. A goddamn good-looking woman. That bastard Glanson, he got himself a nice piece of sweet ass.

That surprised Echo, but it said something about his dead war buddy.

The woman stopped at the bedroom door, started to turn the knob.

"Wait a minute," Echo said. "You aren't going to open that on some roommate with an AK, are you? I told you already, I don't want to have to do horrible things."

She said, "There's nobody here but us." She turned

the knob and opened the door.

Echo fell in behind her as she moved through dangling plastic strips, like what you saw in a supermarket cold room. He moved through the plastic himself, felt a dry heat. A harsh herbal scent lodged in his nose, clutched his throat. He squinted beneath hard yellow lights. When his vision cleared, Echo looked at the room's contents and couldn't help but say: "Goddamn, lady. The fuck is it you got going here? You some kind of kingpin, or am I in a dream?"

Jessie shivered—despite the heat—and said, "It's not a dream, soldier—I'm a fucking kingpin."

THIRTY-THREE

When LaDon reached the front door, he put both palms against it, sat there listening for more shouts. He heard nothing. Could have come from a different apartment, right? No—he was sure he heard Jessie's voice. Fuck. And no gun on him. Nothing but a small pocket knife, a blade he used to open envelopes and take slivers off an apple in the afternoons. He listened some more, thought he heard low voices, but couldn't be sure.

LaDon closed one hand into a fist, pounded on the door. "Jessie, it's me!" No answer. LaDon pounded again. "C'mon, Jessie! I'm outside! Let me in!"

A door opened behind LaDon and he heard a woman say, "That white bitch again." The door slammed. La-Don was about to pound on the door once more, but before he landed another fist, the door swung open to reveal Jessie in an aqua-colored robe, thin fabric clinging tightly to her body. LaDon thought: I might just could get me some tonight.

Echo told Jessie to get dressed and open the fucking door. She ran into the bedroom, grabbed the first thing she saw—a sexy robe she never wore around company, especially not men—and marched down the hall toward the door. She recognized LaDon's voice.

Behind her, Echo followed and moved past her to sit on the couch. The same spot he sat when she came in and got undressed. Out of sight. Where LaDon wouldn't see him.

Jessie didn't want to open the door. Shit, knew she shouldn't open the door. What she considered doing was shouting at LaDon. "Run, LaDon! Call the fucking police!" But Jessie knew that to be the dumbest thing she could do. The police show up and a few people go to prison, including her. Did LaDon have a gun on him? Maybe. She thought to try and signal to him, raise her eyebrows in warning. Or flash him a little skin. LaDon wasn't used to that with her—it might clue him into the situation. Or he might get a hard on. Yeah, knowing LaDon, the hard on was more likely.

Goddammit. And all this because Abbie had the hots for her.

Jessie thought: Fuck love. Fuck it in the ass.

She looked over at Echo while LaDon pounded on the door again.

Echo raised his eyebrows as if to say, go the fuck ahead.

Jessie opened the door. LaDon stood there all big and black, nonthreatening with that coy smile crossing his face. He liked what he saw. Jessie turned, slapped her ass with both hands. She twirled once, moved backwards into the hallway. From the corner of her eye, she saw how Echo shifted on the couch, brought the gun up to center it on LaDon as he walked into the apartment.

She said, "Run, baby," and, as she said it, turned and sprinted toward her grow room.

Behind her, LaDon made a sound in his throat.

Echo went, "The fuck?"

And then Jessie heard three rapid gunshots; they rang as loud as firecrackers in her head.

LaDon liked the way she slapped that ass. Fuck—loved it. He saw her cheeks ripple up to the small of her back, smiled as she twirled for him. See, he thought, I knew she wanted me.

Or, some day she would.

He started in after her, new thoughts running through him about the taste of her skin and the feel of her tongue. And then she said it: "Run, baby."

He gulped and heard a guy's voice to his left. "The fuck?"

LaDon didn't think, he reacted. He crouched and sprinted, dug in like he was playing linebacker back in high school. What did the coaches say? Get low. No, LaDon. Lower. All the way to the ground. And he did get low as he moved through the living area like black lightning.

It surprised him to hear the ringing crash of gunfire. It didn't surprise him that the shots almost plugged him full of holes. The first bullet, from what LaDon could tell, whizzed past his ear. And he was ahead of the shooter by then, moving into the hallway after the blue blur that was Jessie's body. The next two shots plunged into drywall behind him. LaDon swore he felt fire run up from his ass to his head. Nerves and fear, all mixed together like some happy hour highball.

He sprinted after Jessie, dodged right into her grow room. Another bullet zinged by him, filled the space with thunder and malice. Jessie shoved LaDon aside as he stumbled into the room, slammed the door shut behind them. She twisted a deadbolt lock until it clicked, looked at LaDon and said, "Come on in, why don't you?"

He said, "Who the fuck is this gunslinging motherfucker?"

Jessie kneeled beside the door, crossed her arms over her chest. "An old war pal of Abbie's. He's got a good drunk on and he's money hungry."

LaDon bit his bottom lip and shook his head. "Fuck me, Jessie. I knew I should have brought my gun." LaDon waited for a response from her, but there was none. Instead, she stared at him with beautiful and imprecise green eyes.

Outside, in the hallway, the gunman spoke: "You got one minute to come on out of there. Either that, or I'm going to shoot the both of you to shreds. And I promise it'll hurt."

THIRTY-FOUR

Jessie said, "The fuck are we going to do?"

"Wait for the police," LaDon said as he moved backwards into the grow room and through the waist high marijuana plants all soaking up light and nutrients. "Let his ass get shot."

Jessie shook her head as she walked toward him. "Fuck that, LaDon—I am not going to prison."

LaDon watched the door behind Jessie as they moved deeper into the room. What was to stop the fucker from coming into the room? And did Jessie have a gun in here? Maybe—that could sure help. "You got a piece in here, Jessie?"

She put her hands on her hips. "Nope. I keep it in my bedroom."

"I sure wish you had it on you."

Echo's voice came at them through the door. "Thirty seconds, lovebirds. And then I'm coming in." He sounded belligerent and, in an odd way, happy.

LaDon moved aside a dark heavy curtain and poked at cardboard covering the room's lone window.

Jessie said, "It's two floors down. We'll break our necks."

"Better than getting shot in the head."

"Is it?"

LaDon shrugged. God, he didn't believe he left his piece in the Cutlass. Talk about stupid.

Jessie said, "I'm going to talk to him." She turned and started stomping toward the door.

LaDon followed her, said, "Jessie, wait a minute—"

He got cut off by Echo's voice saying, "That's a long ass minute." A moment later gunfire boomed and three shots came through the door.

LaDon heard one shot go by, lodge in the far wall. The other two hit Jessie. She stopped walking and stood still for what felt to LaDon like forever. Odd, to see her standing there touching her midsection, and not being able to see anything more. And then to see her hands come down to her thighs. To see the runny blood dripping from her fingers. To see the red smears grow on the aqua blue robe. LaDon said, "Jessie? You okay?"

And she fell to her knees. She curled over, twisted onto her side. Her face scrunched into a quiet expression that reminded LaDon of a flower before it bloomed. The sounds in the apartment seemed far away—a series of hollow gunshots echoing into nothing. LaDon smelled gunpowder and marijuana. He heard the front door slam and fast footsteps going down the staircase.

He kneeled beside Jessie, tried to meet her eyes with his. She looked distant, deep inside her head. The gunshots were chest and stomach wounds. Bloody, crater-like openings in her tiny woman's body. Blood kept coming and it came out her mouth too, dribbled across her lips. The carpet soaked through and LaDon felt wetness seeping through his slacks. "Jessie? Jess? Girl, you okay? C'mon, now. I need you to keep breathing. I'm going to call the paramedics—I just need you to keep breathing, sister." He shook her, bent down to her mouth, and listened for a small exhalation of breath. Nothing. Not a damn-fucking-thing.

Jessie Jessup was dead.

LaDon sat back on his ass, crossed his arms over his knees. He stared at his dead business partner in disbelief. Shit—he done went to drinks with this woman the other night. They had fucking lunch together. This isn't right. It can't be.

Can it? No. Can't be.

He got back to his knees and shook her again, turned her onto her back. The carpet was dark and wet. Jessie's robe fell open and revealed her naked, wounded body. LaDon covered her again.

"Christ Almighty. Heaven and motherfucking Earth." LaDon did not believe it. He stood and looked around at the marijuana plants. No, I'm not taking all these plants. They're going to have to die. In here with their caretaker. Their creator. He moved through the plants and found the small safe in the closet. He tried a few combinations, but none worked. There was nothing else of value in the closet. He walked past Jessie's body to the grow room door. He could see light from the hallway coming through the bullet holes. He looked back once more at Jessie's body, shook his head. "Goddamn, man. Fuck."

LaDon opened the door and stepped into the hallway. He heard no movement and sensed no other presence. He was certain the gunman was gone. The killer. That's right. The killer was gone. LaDon went into Jessie's bedroom, dug around for money. He checked the dresser, the walk-in closet. He ran through the bathroom drawers and medicine cabinet. Only thing he came up with was an expired Vicodin prescription. He shook the bottle, heard the few pills inside, and decided to take them. He shoved the bottle into his back pocket.

That was it.

He walked back through the hallway, stopped at the grow room. He pushed the door open and stood there, stared at the lifeless woman on the floor. His friend. Shit, LaDon's best friend. Dead as shit on a sidewalk. Now how's that make you feel? LaDon clenched his teeth, scratched beneath his chin. What did Jessie say? The gunman was a friend of Glanson's.

And LaDon had it—this was the fucker he saw downtown with Glanson. When the rasta man laid down the law by shotgun. Holy shit. LaDon shook his head. He took in the sight of Jessie for a last time, tried to keep a mental picture of her laying there in her blood. It hurt, sure. But LaDon needed that image. He thought it might keep him alive somehow.

He walked down the hall, opened the front door, and jogged down the staircase. He walked with urgency through the small apartment complex, came out onto the street. He heard a volley of sirens close by, maybe a few blocks north. Play it cool, LaDon told himself, and you'll be fine.

He passed the two gangbangers again. They still had beers in their hands, but the charcoal grill was empty. No more meat. One guy lifted his chin at LaDon, smirked. The other guy stared. LaDon moved down the street, made a right. Up ahead, he saw his Cutlass glinting gold in the rising moonlight. The sirens sounded closer, but not too close.

LaDon knew he'd make it.

As he reached the car and brought out his keys, La-

Don kept hearing the same thought in his head. It ran through him like a compulsion, a twitch he couldn't control: If you brought your shotgun, maybe Jessie wouldn't be dead. It started with four of us, but two are dead.

Now, it's only me and him.

THE TWO

THIRTY-FIVE

Echo walked a few blocks west, turned and started to jog. After a mile or so he was winded. He reached a rundown business district and started walking. He didn't know whether the police knew what he looked like. Could be that Jessie and her big black friend called the police. Echo didn't know. He just couldn't be sure. All that weed in her place though, Echo didn't think Jessie wanted the police involved. No, how could she?

Echo spotted a dive bar ahead, the blinking neon sign labeling the place as Marky's. Echo nodded at the doorman, found himself inside staring at wood paneling, Grolsch and Rolling Rock signs, and a small bar with a portly woman on duty behind it. Two customers on one end. Both old guys with white hair and half-empty rocks glasses cradled in their hands.

Echo went ahead and sat a little ways down the bar, where he wouldn't have to acknowledge the old timers. He nodded at the portly woman as she looked him up and down. "You mind if I get a bottle of Bud? And maybe a shot of Evan Williams?"

She nodded and popped the beer. Echo drank like he'd washed up off a desert island. She poured him the shot and squinted. "Never seen you around here," she said.

Echo grinned. "Got a friend who lives nearby. It's my first time in." He motioned at the entrance, the door man standing there like a prison guard. "You get a big crowd on weekdays?"

The portly bartender smirked at Echo, sneezed without covering her nose. "Ramon's here in case anybody decides to fuck around. My advice to you? Don't fuck around."

Echo nodded and thought, I will most definitely not fuck around. If I can help it. She moved off down the bar and Echo shot his whiskey, grunted as it burned his throat and belly. He stared at his hands, the right one shaking there on top of the bar. He tried to pin it down with his left.

Nothing doing. What's the matter, man? You don't even know you hit anybody.

Besides, you've killed people before—in the Eye-Rack. You killed lots of people.

Except Echo did think he hit somebody. Maybe the girl. He heard the big black dude say something to her after the shots. And it sounded frantic. So, what if you did hit her? Echo raised his eyebrows at the bartender, pointed at his drinks. She came back and gave him another round.

So, I hit her. That don't mean she's taking the dirt nap. No, there were sirens close to us and she got help if she needed it. He snorted down the whiskey shot, chased it with beer. Wait a minute. Fuck all that noise. How about the fact I didn't get any goddamn money. Except for the few bills he already got from Jessie, Echo got nothing. He came out of there with maybe two grand.

Chump change. Fuck.

Alright. What now? Another drink, Echo thought.

Then I need to get back to my place, grab a go-bag. I need to get out of this city. He came out and tried to make a run with Glanson, but now Glanson was dead—along with his lady friend—and the cops weren't dummies. Soon enough, they'd get Echo in a room and start asking him pointed questions. Best to avoid all that.

Echo stood and walked past the two old timers, entered the restroom. He locked the door and screwed his face at the smell of rotting shit. You can't get that smell out of those old restrooms. Once it's there, you need to get used to it. Echo looked at himself in the mirror, saw that his hand kept shaking. What is it with you, motherfucker? He ran the sink and soaked his hair. Tried to calm himself by rubbing water in his eyes and all around his face.

Yeah, he needed to skip town.

Echo left the bathroom, finished his drinks at the bar.

"You want another one, buddy?"

Echo shook his head and coughed. He shoved his shaking right hand into a pocket and turned to leave. "Thanks for the drinks."

"Hey, wait a minute. What the fuck?"

Echo brushed past the door man, heard the bartender yell: "Ramon! Stop that guy! He didn't pay!" Echo ran across the street, slid into a dark alley. He ran the alley's length, came out in front of a two-pump gas station. He crossed the station's lot and turned a corner, found himself on another high-density residential street.

Echo decided to jog. He made it one block and heard shouting in the distance. The door man, maybe. And that made Echo think about the bartender. She said he didn't pay. Even though he had a couple thou in his pockets. True, and somehow that put Echo on another thought.

He didn't get paid—not like Glanson promised. He spotted a lowered Honda Civic on the street, late nineties model. He stopped and checked the street. Nobody in sight, though he heard music in a few places—the ceaseless thump of too strong bass—and animated voices in a nearby yard. Right, he thought, I didn't get paid.

That's what matters—I did not get paid.

He remembered the image from Glanson's cell phone, the one he saw at the restaurant. The first time he sees Glanson in, what, two and a half years? And Glanson whips out this image, his boss standing in all this fucking money. Looked like millions. And here I am, Echo told himself, running away from this thing and not getting paid. Fuck the fuck out of that. He shook his head, checked the street once more. When he was ready, Echo lifted a boot and kicked in the driver's side rear window. There was a short crashing sound, but no alarm. He reached inside the car, unlocked and opened the front door. He got behind the wheel, started yanking wires from beneath the steering column. Twenty seconds later, the car started and running fine, Echo made an unprotected left onto the next street and headed toward the nearest freeway ramp.

He was driving, but he wasn't going anywhere. No fucking way. Echo needed to get paid.

That image kept drilling into his brain. All that fucking money. Sitting there in some storage unit.

Yes, sir. Echo smiled, checked his mirrors. You can bet your skinny ass—I'm getting paid.

If it's the last thing I do.

THIRTY-SIX

LaDon didn't remember backing the Cutlass into his normal spot outside The Zip Zap Bar.

But there he was, a black man with blood on his hands, sitting outside a dive bar waiting for a reason not to go inside and take a drink. And another drink. And a few more after that.

He had a simple thought: how did I let this happen?

Sirens sounded behind him, a few miles north. And the police and news choppers droned over the city like mechanized insects. All the noise, LaDon knew, centered on a woman's lifeless body in a shitty Mid-City apartment. Her and her six figures worth of marijuana plants.

LaDon dialed a number, sat watching drunks stagger out of the bar. A few people out front smoking, most of them folks LaDon knew from way back. Matter of fact, they probably wondered what the fuck he was doing in the Cutlass. No music on the radio or nothing. Let them wonder, he thought. Fuck it.

LaDon didn't have to listen to the digital cell phone ring for long—Moonie answered on the third chime, a little alcohol and weed coming though in his voice.

"Yo, this Moonie."

"It's me, man."

"Yo, LaDon. What you doing up so late? I thought you were all white collar and shit, sleeping at a decent hour and using a calculator all day."

LaDon said, "I sound like I want to laugh right now?"

Moonie didn't say shit to that.

"What I want to know, you get on that man I told you about? The security dude?"

Moonie coughed. "Picked him up this afternoon, after you and me had a bite."

"And?" LaDon switched the phone from one ear to the other.

"And," Moonie said, "I followed his ass around for six hours. One part of the city to the next, like the man's delivering smiles to every shit neighborhood in San Diego. He about put me down on skid row, all the gas I got to buy. Know what? I want a little more than—"

"Moonie, do me a favor, will you?"

"LaDon, you know I—"

"Shut your junkie motherfucking mouth."

Moonie obeyed the order but breathed heavy over the line. Like he just got done doing push-ups.

"Where in the fuck he end up?"

Moonie said, "Down to the South Bay. Couple exits before the border crossing. One of those storage unit joints. Parked out front, went inside with a bunch of black gym bags—they were full—and came out without 'em. After that, I followed his ass to a poker room in the Southeast. That joint next to the fried chicken shop off of...what is it?"

"Off Home Ave?"

"That's it, yeah."

LaDon sighed. He switched the phone to his other ear again. The smokers out front of the bar went inside and the parking lot was empty and quiet, except for the sound of LaDon's own heavy breathing. He tasted the insides of his mouth and closed one eye with deep thought.

"You okay, LaDon?"

"No, man."

"Yo, LaDon, what happened?"

"Jessie got popped."

"You got to be playing with me. Jessie? She dead?"

LaDon said, "Crickets."

"Fuck, man. I'm sorry to hear that."

"She knew the risks."

Moonie coughed some more. He cleared his throat and said, "I guess that's true."

LaDon kept his mouth shut for a minute. He wanted to think about all that money. See, thinking about it made him feel right. Made him feel like the money was the whole point of this—there wasn't anything else. Not when you got down to the bottom of it. All the way down into the dark parts of it. Jessie was dead, but it was still about the money.

Greenbacks and lettuce and dolla-dolla bills.

How to get it.

How to hold it.

How to hide it.

But mostly how to get it. Yeah, LaDon thought, I want that fucking money. He sniffed hard through his nose and sighed. "Moonie, you free tomorrow? I got another job for you."

"Yeah, LaDon. I could be free. I'll tell you something though: I'm sorry about your girl, but I'll be fucked in the ass if I'm going to waste a whole day for seventy-five bucks. I want double, brother. I want over-fucking-time.

That's nonnegotiable, LaDon."

LaDon said, "You're saying you want one-fifty for a whole day's work?"

"Damn right. Time is money. And my time's valuable as fuck. I'm a busy man."

"I'll make it better than all that. I only need you for a couple hours. I'll give you the one-fifty."

"Sounds good to me. Tell me when and where—I'm there."

"I'll call you tomorrow," LaDon said. "Oh, and Moonie..."

"Yeah?"

"You're wrong about this. Time ain't money. Money's money, Moonie. Remember I told you that." LaDon ended the call and sat there in the still silent parking lot. A few minutes later he went into The Zip Zap Bar for a drink. And another one after that. And another.

LaDon drank all night. Like he'd just been to a funeral for a friend.

THIRTY-SEVEN

Echo made it down to the coast, parked a block east of Garnet, the main drag with its bars and overpriced restaurants. He wiped the stolen Honda down with his hooded sweatshirt. He'd leave it there and find something else to drive when he needed it. Out on Garnet, Echo went into the first frat boy bar he saw—Coast Tap House. He sat at one of the high cocktail tables set back from the bar. There was a pro basketball game playing on the bank of flat-screen televisions above the bar. Echo watched that until his waitress, a skinny girl with bangs over her eyes, asked him what he wanted.

"I'll take the cheapest beer you have. And a shot of tequila."

"Blue Ribbon and Cuervo go for eight bucks—it's a special." She used a finger to lift her bangs and squint at him. A nice-looking girl. Too young for Echo, maybe. But pretty and with a bell-shaped ass in her short plaid skirt. Looked like a faux-Catholic girl thing she had going.

"Will you take a shot with me?"

She smiled with one side of her mouth. "Sure."

When she came back, they clinked shot glasses and Echo said, "Here's to us, and fuck everybody else."

They drank and smiled at each other.

"I'm Tessa. Just wave if you need another drink."

"Will do, Tessa." Echo watched the sweet ass vanish in the crowd. The place wasn't so busy for a Friday night, but it was still early for the college crowd. There were a few open spots at the bar and Echo could make out the sound of the basketball game over the slurred conversation. He planned to have a few drinks and head home, maybe take the waitress with him. Or convince her to meet up with him when her shift ended. Beneath the table, he counted the roll of cash in his pocket—a little more than two grand in hundreds, fifties, and twenties. He sipped his beer and tried to feel guilty about shooting Jessie. It didn't work, but it made him remember coming home from the war.

Walking into the house where he grew up, his mom a few years older with that gray hair cut above her shoulders, and sitting down at the kitchen table. Drinking that too strong coffee and waiting for the questions to come. Waiting for Ray to get home from his job at the electric company, to drape his tool belt across the back of the couch and say, "Hey, Donnie—back so soon, huh? You got the rent money?" Waiting for anything normal to happen now that he was back. Except it wasn't like that. It wasn't one bit normal. His mom pouring more and more coffee. Offering that powdered creamer like they had in Eye-Rack. Fuck that. What Echo did is say, "I'm going out, Mom." And he gave her a kiss on the forehead and got on his motorcycle.

Ride west, young man. Ride west.

Never went back to see Mom and now here he was: sitting in some frat boy bar and getting turned on by a college girl. And wanted for murder soon enough. If not for the woman—Jessie—it'd be for Glanson. And that big black dude coming after him. If Echo knew anything, he knew the guy was a serious type, somebody you didn't jerk around. What Echo should have done was kick open the door and shoot them both.

Alright, so what? You want the money, don't you?

Yeah, I want the money. But...I can get my ass on a bus and head back to the Midwest. Ride the fucker for twenty hours, step off in the three-stoplight town of my youth. Walk out into Main Street and past the diner and the library and the barbershop. Walk right up to my mom's house, past Ray's electric company pickup truck, knock on the door. Fucking smile like a clown when she opens the door. "Hey, Mom...I'm sorry. I just had some things to work out. But I'm fine now. See?" Go into the living room, flop down on the couch and start watching *The Price is Right*. Sit there with Mom and guess the price of a new set of silverware, an economy car, a vacation to the fucking Maldives. Listen to Mom talk my ear off about how Miss Lewis told so and so off down at the Sunday potluck. And didn't I know that Pastor John had a new woman from that Thailand place? Hear the whole spiel about his high school buddies moving up at the electric company, making Ray feel like shit because he kept failing the test for his promotion. Yeah, I want the money. But...I can do that if I really want. Disappear back into the old me.

All this gave Echo a taste like vomit in his mouth.

He waved at the waitress and she brought another beer and shot. He shoved the tequila toward her. "It's on me. Go ahead." She took it and Echo copped a feel as she ran off to her other customers. He drank beer and stared at the basketball game some more. What, then?

Go follow Glanson's boss until he went back to the storage unit? Sure, Echo. And bring a loaded gun and...

Take that motherfucking money.

Fuck all this waiting around. All this amateur hour bullshit.

The waitress came back and leaned toward him with her elbows on the table.

Echo said, "What time you get off tonight?"

"Midnight."

Echo nodded and said, "Hour and a half."

"That's right, smarty pants."

"Tell you what: Bring me another drink and I'll hang out. Let me walk you home."

"I drive home," she said.

"I'll drive you then...Tessa."

The waitress gave him fuck-me eyes and said, "I think we'll take a taxi."

Echo said, "We can take the fast train to hell, for all I care. Long as we're together."

"You say that to all the girls?"

"Just the ones I want to fuck." He expected her to tell him off after that line, maybe spill his beer in his lap.

But she didn't.

Instead, Tessa the waitress said, "It's a good line. Don't use it too much or it'll go sour."

THIRTY-EIGHT

LaDon staggered out of The Zip Zap Bar. He stood in the parking lot, dug through his pockets for a Black & Mild. Came up empty. He nodded at Zim who came out and locked the bar's front door. It was two-thirty in the morning—a dark quiet night around them.

"You got a smoke I can bum, Zim?"

Zim found his cigarettes, passed one to LaDon.

They lit up and watched the empty city street.

Zim said, "I got some more of your money over where we talked about. Only half of it though. I'm trying out a new girl. She gonna take the other half on Monday, red-eye flight out of LAX."

LaDon's hearing felt all fogged up, like Zim was talking to him underwater. He shook his head and smoked the cigarette, let the night air touch his face and neck.

Zim slapped LaDon's back. "Man, what's up with you tonight? The other day, I got you in here handing me a bag of money, all worried about getting it into the bank. Now, you're drunk as ever, looking like you saw a ghost or some shit."

LaDon caught all that—it cut right the fuck through his buzz. He leaned against the wall, stared sidelong at his gold Cutlass while he talked. "Ran into some trouble tonight, Zim. Me and Jessie. Ran into some big trouble. It's bad, too."

"What kind of trouble?"

"Jessie's dead."

"The fuck she is. C'mon, man—don't play with me." Zim lit another smoke with the nub of his first, dropped the butt and crushed it with his boot. He dragged and exhaled. "You had too many gimlets, you big ass motherfucker."

LaDon shrugged, sniffed through one clear nostril. "It's a shame, to watch a woman like that go over to the other side. A damn shame. And over some bullshit, too."

"You're not fucking with me."

"No, Zim. I'm not fucking with you."

"Goddamn—what the fuck happened, LaDon?"

LaDon shook his head. He leaned all the way against the wall, stared up at the sky slick with low cloud cover and bathed in city light. "You don't want to hear none of it. Trust me."

Zim stood with his mouth hanging open, a small cloud of cigarette smoke drifting from between his lips. He tapped the cigarette against a thigh. "I mean, shit. I seen her last week. She come in here and order a couple martinis. Sat there drinking and watching *Wheel of Fortune* on the TV. Matter of fact, she got one hard puzzle. What was it?" He thought for a few seconds, snapped his fingers. "'I'm going for broke.' That was the phrase. I remember we both laughed and—"

"I beat down that pimp." LaDon gulped air, frowned.

Zim shuffled his feet, looked off down the street. "Who you mean?"

"The white girl that was in here the other day."

"Yeah?"

"I tracked down her man, beat his ass into the ground."

Zim rubbed his left cheek, took a long drag from the cigarette.

LaDon finished his and dropped it. He let it sit there and burn, a pale red smudge on the pavement.

Zim said, "You getting back into all that, LaDon?"

"I'm not back into anything. I'm just..."

"Just beating pimps down and bragging about it."

LaDon shrugged again and let his head hang to one side.

"That business with the gangbangers and the shotgun and the—"

"I still have that gun. Matter of fact, it's in the—"

Zim lifted a hand and said, "I do not want to hear this, LaDon."

They stood in silence for a while. LaDon liked how the city got quiet at night. Not dead completely, but subdued. That's what he'd call it. He heard a car engine a few blocks down, a motorcycle revving much farther away. He stood up straight, smoothed down his pants. The buzz was almost gone. He felt cleaner. More in control. Jessie was out of his mind.

Zim said, "You okay to drive, partner?"

"Yeah. You want a lift home?"

Zim shook his head. "I'm alright. It's only two blocks. I'll see you."

They slapped hands and LaDon said, "Be good."

Zim walked through the parking lot and made a left, disappeared behind some old buildings along the street. The cloud cover hung over the street like a lazy fog. It got quieter.

LaDon shuffled across the parking lot toward the Cutlass. He ran a finger through the condensation on the hood. Surprised him how cold it was this night. He pulled out his keys, had no trouble unlocking the driver's side door. He fell into the seat, switched on the car. He liked the Cutlass' pleasant whirring sound, the small vibrations that ran from the engine, through the floor-board, and up through the seat into his ass. Not a perfect car, but it felt right to LaDon. Like he was meant to drive it. LaDon pulled out of the parking lot, made a right with the intention of driving to his apartment. It wasn't until he made a left at the next intersection that LaDon felt the round tip of a gun press firmly behind his right ear.

"You get a minute, I want you to flip a bitch. We headed in the wrong direction."

LaDon recognized the voice: It was Ginny's pimp.

Eddie.

THIRTY-NINE

Echo snorted the line of coke—a fat line, too—off Tessa's bare chest. He shook his head and made a sound like a wet dog, bent his head to bite her purple nipples.

"Ouch, wild man." Tessa squirmed beneath Echo, grabbed at his junk. "You going to put that thing in me? Or am I going to handle all this myself?"

A second later, Echo slid into her and worked at it for a cool two minutes. He tried to stop and let things rest, but Tessa dug her nails into his ass and moaned. He let go with a long whoof in his throat, collapsed on top of her.

She ran her hands up and down his spine. "You think you can do that again in fifteen?"

"I fucking hope so. It's a waste of good coke if I don't."

"Just the coke, huh?" She sat up on the bed, pulled her hair back into a ponytail.

"The pussy, too."

"Well, I'm glad it comes in a close second." She put her hand between her legs and started to rub. A short gasp left her throat. She whimpered.

Echo put his hand on top of hers. "Give me five minutes—I promise I'll be ready."

Tessa stopped and said, "You fucking better keep that promise."

They lay there smoking while Echo tried to recover. They were in Tessa's studio apartment, a four-hundred-square-foot affair without a stove. She had a small refrigerator, a microwave, and a sink. A tiny bathroom opposite the front door. No television or computer. Bare bones and about as quaint as a nowhere motel room. Looked like she was passing through. Or headed out soon.

Echo said, "You don't keep much of a home."

"I'm a law student. It's either work or the law library downtown. What do you want from me?"

"Shit, I don't know. A picture on the wall, maybe. A fucking dead orchid on the window sill."

"I bet your place is so much better." She blew smoke at him, reached for the baggie of coke on the nightstand. She dug some powder out with her thumb, snorted it.

"Some goddamn lawyer you're going to be."

"I never said I wanted to be a lawyer."

It surprised Echo. He felt himself stir around the groin. "What then?"

"DEA," she said. "You believe it?"

"Jesus. What about all the lie detector shit they do? How you going to get around that?"

Tessa laughed. She licked her fingers. "What kind of DEA agent will I be if I can't cheat a lie detector test? Besides, how am I supposed to know what drugs do to somebody, you know, if I don't do them myself? Call it research."

"Research..."

"Yeah."

Echo sat up in the bed, scratched his chin. "Hey, let

me ask you something. If I came across, say, a million bucks—and it's drug money—what can I do with it? Like, I can't put it in a bank and—"

"Not here you can't. Not without the IRS waxing your ass."

"Right—so do I just carry this cash around with me for the next ten years?"

"You need to wash it. You need to find a legitimate business, something clean, and work that money into the cash flow. This way, it all comes out clean."

Echo groaned. He didn't like that. "Isn't there anything else?"

"Get it to the Caribbean, the Cayman Islands. Some place like that. But a million bucks," Tessa said, "is a shit lot of money. Not like it fits down your underpants."

Echo nodded and said, "But I can take it little by little. It was in that movie, Tarantino…"

"*Jackie Brown*," Tessa said.

"Right." He snapped his fingers.

"She got caught in that one. That's what starts the movie…I'm just saying." Tessa squeezed her right boob, lifted it to her lips and sucked on her nipple until it got hard.

Echo watched her and licked his lips. "I wouldn't know what to do with it, all that money."

Tessa stopped sucking and said, "It's a problem, but it's a good problem. I'd just put it somewhere. When I needed it, I'd keep going back to the well."

"Like a storage unit?"

"Sure…Why not?"

Another thing Echo didn't like. But he could deal with that: going out and taking the money, moving it to another storage facility. And waiting for some legitimate way to wash it. Shit, he might get himself a Laundromat. Or a dry cleaning business. A fucking taco cart.

Whatever the fuck it took to clean his money.

Tessa pinched her hard purple nipple, placed her other hand between her legs.

Echo said, "You're fucking crazy, you know that?"

Tessa grunted and said, "Is that little thing of yours getting big yet?"

Echo reached down and touched himself. "Yeah, it is."

"I'm in charge this time," she said, "and you're going to do what I say."

FORTY

They drove for about fifteen blocks along El Cajon Avenue, LaDon taking them past taco shops and smog check stations, a pho joint or three. All the shitty bars closed down for the night. They got all green lights, but LaDon had trouble staying in his lane. He tried both hands. It didn't quite work like he wanted. The Cutlass swung in and out of both lanes.

Eddie kept that gun pressed behind LaDon's ear. When the Cutlass' tires caught road Braille again, he said, "Man, what the fuck is wrong with you? You got this bomb ride and you don't know how to drive?"

LaDon said, "I'm buzzed."

"Oh, I get it. You're fucking drunk."

LaDon watched Eddie through the rearview mirror, saw his eyes dart back and forth, those thoughts running from ear to ear. LaDon steered into the other lane again—a more pronounced swerve. "I'm fine to drive, man. Shit."

"Pull the fuck over."

LaDon pulled into a strip mall parking lot, put the Cutlass in park.

Eddie put the gun to the back of LaDon's neck. "Scoot your ass over. Put your seatbelt on. I want your hands in your lap when you finish. And don't fucking move."

LaDon did as instructed.

Eddie reached forward and popped open the driver's side door. He pushed the seat forward and climbed out, all the while with the gun leveled on LaDon. He bent down, smiled, and said, "Nope, I don't mind one bit if I do the driving. Thanks for asking." He fell into the driver's seat and used his left hand to point the gun across his body at LaDon.

LaDon knew right away it was the same gun he passed to Ginny, a .45. Something Eddie got off the street. No serial number or traceable history.

Eddie used his right hand to steer. Kept that .45 on LaDon.

"Where we going, man?"

Eddie shrugged and ran his tongue across his upper lip. "Going to pick up my girl."

"She didn't leave, huh?"

They passed two police cruisers parked side by side at a twenty-four-hour gas station. The two cops parked facing in opposite directions—so they could shoot the shit. Neither cruiser moved as Eddie steered the Cutlass deeper into the city.

Eddie said, "Man, all she did was pull my car around the block, wait till you and your lady took off. Came right back to pick my ass up."

LaDon studied Eddie's face. It was still plump in the lower half, but it looked like he had medication for the swelling; he had some able hands to mend his ass. La-Don sighed and said, "She wasn't my lady. She was my friend."

"My experience, and take this from a bonafide pimp,

you stay too long in the friend zone...You're asking for a woman to smoke your ass, take advantage of you."

"I appreciate your advice, but you don't know shit."

Eddie chuckled and shook his head. "Oh, I know some stuff. Let me tell you." He slowed for a yellow light, stopped as it turned red. He checked the mirrors—still no cops. "A woman needs to know where she stands with a man. That's how you keep shit under control. You let her—"

"Like I said, you don't know shit about me or my friend." LaDon put a knife edge in his voice, felt the anger at the back of his throat. "Pimp or not. You don't know shit."

"Hey, whatever buddy," Eddie said. The light turned green and Eddie pulled through the intersection, cruised slowly down a rundown stretch of mattress stores and thrift shops. "There she is—roll down your window."

LaDon squinted and saw Ginny on the corner. She had one hand cocked high on her hip, above a way-too-short skirt and come-fuck-me boots. Two other girls stood near her, both in similar outfits. Ginny was taller than both. LaDon said, "Those other two yours?"

"Fucking-A."

LaDon rolled down his window as Eddie slid the Cutlass to the curb.

Ginny bent down to peer inside the car.

Eddie grinned and said, "How much for a pump and suck?"

Ginny shook her head. "For you it's free, baby." Her mascara-caked eyes lit on LaDon. "Your friend though, it'll cost him a c-note."

LaDon poked a cheek with his tongue before he said, "A c-note for a worn out whore like you? I wouldn't pay twenty dollars to fuck you raw." He saw black flash in his eyes before the .45 swiped across his forehead. The blow gave LaDon an instant headache and he sank deeper into his seat. He felt saliva hit his right cheek as Ginny cussed and spat on him. LaDon swam up from the oppressive persuasion of a blackout and stared bullets at Ginny. The fuck was she doing? He pulled himself up in the seat, kept his mouth shut.

"You want to keep talking, I'm all for it." Eddie leaned against the driver's side door, kept the .45 resting peaceful and silent in his lap. "I like to hit people." He smiled. "In case you haven't noticed."

LaDon didn't respond. Instead, he thought about how to get out of this. Maybe there wasn't a way. Maybe Jessie got done, and now it was LaDon's turn. It'd be unexpected, sure. But why the hell not? All of us get done in the end. It's a promise, the only one God always keeps.

Eddie shook his head and said, "Get in the back, Ginny. I'm about to show this motherfucker what happens when people fuck with me or my girls."

LaDon followed Ginny with his eyes as she swayed in front of the Cutlass, came around to the driver's side. Eddie climbed out and let her into the back seat. He got back in and revved the Cutlass' engine. Ginny's smell filled the car: Vaseline and hand sanitizer. Drugstore perfume and the unseen vapor of ten thousand hand jobs. Cigarettes and cheap gin.

LaDon said, "Here we go again."

FORTY-ONE

When Echo woke up, it was four-thirty in the morning. He checked his phone and watched Tessa's naked belly rise and fall for fifteen minutes. What? Was he going to marry this girl? Fuck, no. Why the fuck was he still in her bed? He didn't know.

Another thing he did that, maybe, made little or no sense.

Alright. So, get the fuck out of here.

Echo swung out of the bed, dressed as quiet as possible, and started for the apartment's front door. He spotted Tessa's purse on a small, lopsided dresser. He stopped, turned to look at her. She slept with one arm over her eyes, like she passed out under a bright sun. Her nipples pointed straight at the ceiling, and her legs were crossed. Echo reached for the purse, a small clutch with a silver buckle, and opened it. He found three twenty-dollar bills, an ID, and some credit cards. He also found a square key fob with a key that came out when he clicked a button. Looked like Tessa had herself a new vehicle. Echo took the money and the key before he slipped out into the early morning light.

They weren't far from the bar where he met Tessa and Echo needed some exercise.

He tightened his boot laces and started jogging.

* * *

Echo found Tessa's car in the parking lot adjacent to the bar. He clicked the alarm button and the horn honked twice. She drove a black Elantra—mid-2000s—with tinted windows and a CD player. Inside, Echo adjusted the driver's seat and mirrors. He figured Tessa wouldn't report the car stolen until she left work that evening.

He planned to be gone by then. In another boosted car.

In the window visor, Echo found a sheaf of compact discs. He chose Tupac—"All Eyez on Me"—and slipped it into the player. As Echo pulled onto the main drag and headed toward the freeway, the soft thump of bass filled the car—he bobbed his head to the beat.

First thing he did was swing by the pot lady's apartment. He slowed on her street and idled past her apartment building's walkway. There was yellow crime scene tape draped in an X shape across the staircase leading to her apartment, but no police presence. Alright, then. He kept driving, made a right at the next cross street, circled back around to look again. As he pulled alongside the apartment again, Echo thought about the big black dude.

What about him?

Is he coming after me? Not if he doesn't know where I am—it's impossible.

Echo stopped, sat there in a stolen car and stared at the yellow crime scene tape. I'm not going in there again. No way. No reason to go inside—fuck all the pot. The cops got it by now. And did they talk to the big black guy? Maybe. Could be. Or did the big black guy take off? How does somebody answer questions about all that pot. Echo knew it wasn't legal. No way in hell. Echo remembered Glanson talking about the lady, how she had that dispensary. How it brought in mad cash. And wasn't there...Shit, yes. How she worked with a guy named, what was it? Don? Something like that. Or maybe it was LaRon—that could be.

Echo took his foot off the brake, let the Elantra slide toward the stop sign. He rolled though the stop and accelerated toward El Cajon Boulevard. His thoughts ran as fast as the car. He made a right, changed lanes. LaDon—that was the big black guy's name. And he worked with Jessie. LaDon so and so. A big tough motherfucker, Glanson said. And the dispensary was near a bar Echo knew. Where him and Glanson met on the night they did the first job.

When Echo killed that unlucky old fucker.

Glanson told Echo enough that, if he needed, he could find the place. Shit, businesses have signs, right? No doubt about that—even drug dealers need to advertise.

All Echo needed to do was go to that bar and work outward in a grid. Drive all the streets and keep his eyes open. He needed to find the dispensary and wait for LaDon. The other thing was Glanson's boss worked for the place. He picked up their money. Every day? Probably not. But at least once a week. And once a week is all you need when you're about to rip a motherfucker off.

What Echo wanted was to watch LaDon and to follow Abel. See what the mean motherfucker is all about, what he does. Pick up the money man and take him down— both the people Echo needed to see, and both in one place. Or would be in one place.

Yeah, he told himself, I'm on a recon mission. And this shit is on, motherfucker. It's on.

FORTY-TWO

"What you thought," Eddie said, "is that a bitch don't want to be a bitch." He merged onto the freeway—they headed south. Up ahead, the downtown buildings glowed in the night. They moved into the fast lane through almost nonexistent traffic. "But I'm here to tell you: my bitches don't just want to be bitches, they love to be bitches." Eddie laughed at himself.

LaDon watched the city lights as they approached. He spotted the El Cortez Hotel sign, blinking red high above the freeway. He sniffed hard through one nostril and scratched his neck. Ginny's scent hung in the Cutlass, like a food aroma taunting him late at night. "You see these girls like dogs, am I right?" LaDon didn't look at Eddie. He watched red taillights whir past as the Cutlass overtook them, caught sight of the bay bridge sweeping like a wave to North Island.

Ginny spoke up from the back seat. "We're not like dogs. We're like—what are they called?—racing horses. Like they have in Del Mar. Or Santa Anita."

Eddie said, "Thoroughbreds, baby. You're like thoroughbreds."

It was LaDon's turn to laugh. And he did. He stopped himself and rubbed his chin.

Eddie said to him: "You think all this shit is funny, but you the one about to wake up in hell. You know, I noticed that about guys...They think it's funny until they wake up in hell."

LaDon looked over at Eddie, saw the gun in his lap. "Man, you talk like we're living in black and white. It's fucking crazy."

"What's that mean?"

Ginny said, "He means the movies. You talk like you're in a movie."

Eddie said, "You know the last movie I saw? Fucking Superman Gets Another Hard On or whatever. I ain't versed in all the film scholarship out there or nothing, but I know there's got to be other stories out there besides Superman. You can't tell me that's all there is."

LaDon said, "Film talk with Eddie the pimp. That what this is?"

"Tell me there ain't better stories on the street." He glanced sidelong at LaDon, painted him with those hard, round eyes. Like what he did to his girls. His bitches.

Ginny said, "I've seen some shit. I could write about a hundred movies."

Eddie steered across three lanes, piloted them toward an exit ramp.

"Like this, for an example," LaDon said. "How a street pimp and a dumb fuck try to kill a mean-ass black man. That a plot you can get behind?"

"I can get behind a lot of shit," Eddie said. "Except that bit about trying to kill a black man. You and me both know, I'm going to kill your ass. There's nothing you can do about it."

"You never said we'd kill him." Ginny's voice wavered—she sounded hunched up in her seat.

"Well, baby. You see it written down somewhere I got to tell you my plans?"

"No."

"Fucking right. I say we need to kill this fucker and—"

LaDon twisted in the seat, lunged for the steering wheel.

Eddie lifted the gun and planted it between LaDon's wide eyes. He smirked and said, "Not so fast, big man. Not unless you want a makeover for your funeral."

"Christ," Ginny said.

LaDon shrank back into the passenger seat. He loosened his seatbelt and closed his eyes. Without looking at Eddie, LaDon said, "I got to try."

"Yeah, you do." Eddie slowed the car and they made a left onto a freeway overpass.

LaDon opened his eyes when the road got rough. He heard the creak of the shocks and the persistent rattle of gravel against the car's undercarriage. They were rolling through orchard trees. Looked like oranges to LaDon, but he couldn't see too well through the darkness. "You already got the grave dug, or what?"

Eddie grunted. "I like to plan things out, sure. Don't you worry—I picked a nice spot."

LaDon nodded. He closed his eyes again.

Eddie sighed and started talking like he didn't have an audience: "I still remember this boy out in Rolando. College punk Sadie picked up off University and Euclid, near the old Kmart. What he did, he tried to get her to suck him off after they got through. Double dipping, you know? I'm watching from a fast food joint across the street, Taco Bell if I remember. Used to sit there and munch on chips and salsa while my girls—my *bitches*—

did their thing. Right there in the alley between a pet store and the adult bookstore over that way. You know it? Anyway, I see it all go down: I see Sadie lead him by the hand into the shadows. There's a yellow light coming from above, one of those security lights, and I see her lift her skirt, pull down her panties. He does his thing—it don't take long—and when she goes to take his money… this motherfucker shoves Sadie to the ground. He bends over, gets a grip on her hair and, well, you can imagine the rest. I'm walking across the street as soon as I see it. What I used to have was a knock-off Glock, something you get on the street to scare your homies. I pull the thing out and I hear Sadie groaning. The guy's got her on her knees and he's trying to put his dick in her mouth and I just, I fired the fucking gun. Right at his throat. You get surprised the way it is—not all dramatic like the movies."

LaDon's thoughts flashed on Jessie, all that blood on her hands. The red-black liquid pooling around her.

"What happens is they just fall. Like a napkin you dropped. There we were in the dark. And I aimed that sorry excuse for a Glock and I fired." Eddie made a smooch sound with his lips.

"Boom," LaDon said.

"Shocka locka," Eddie said.

Ginny was quiet.

Thirty seconds later, Eddie slowed the Cutlass and came to a stop.

It was too dark to see much, but LaDon thought he made out waving orange trees. He heard the soft sound of leaves touching each other, shimmering, falling to the dark-soiled ground.

Eddie looked at him and smiled. "This is it," he said. "Time to say goodnight."

* * *

Eddie waved the gun at LaDon. "Go on around to the trunk—I already popped it."

They were standing outside the car. Ginny stood behind Eddie, stared at LaDon with her hands on her hips, one foot tapping the dirt. LaDon saw now they were in an orchard. Oranges, he thought—those low trees with big bushy branches, and the fruit hanging off them like large juicy testicles. Better here than some Mid-City shit hole, LaDon told himself. Oh, well. He walked around to the trunk, turned to face Eddie as he came around the car.

Eddie rubbed at the plump part of his cheek. The gun hung loosely in his other hand, though it was pointed in a general way at LaDon. The pimp looked younger somehow, like a kid who puts a mask on for Halloween. He's not what he says he is, but something else.

LaDon crossed his arms and said, "You're the real bitch here."

"How you figure that?"

"You probably ain't even shot a squirrel. I can see it in your face. I bet you don't even know how to pimp, not for real. You just got lucky, found you some girls who don't know any better."

"Fuck you, black man."

"Alright then," LaDon said. "Let's get it on. Show off for your lady there."

Ginny said, "You don't have to prove nothing, Eddie."

Eddie shook his head, half-turned to Ginny. "Speak when spoken to," he said. "By me."

"Sorry, Eddie."

"Me too," LaDon said. "I'm sorry, too. I'm sorry for

every time you look at yourself and see a street punk, a no good piece of shit. Not to mention, you're one ugly ass pimp. And you too," LaDon glared at Ginny, "with your broken ass teeth and your stretched out—"

"Quiet down, motherfucker." Eddie shook his head. An annoyed gesture, nothing to say the comment hit him. Not in a way that mattered.

"Don't talk to me or my man that way."

Eddie half-turned. "What I say about talking?"

"My bad." Ginny bit the nails on one hand.

Eddie turned back to LaDon and said, "Look, what's your name again?"

"LaDon."

"LaDon what?" He gestured with the gun.

"LaDon Marcus Garvey Charles."

"Fuck me. What kind of name is that?"

LaDon uncrossed his arms, put his right foot up on the Cutlass' bumper. "The kind of name your momma gives you when your daddy's a black panther."

"Is that supposed to scare me?"

"No, but you asked."

Eddie shuffled his feet, switched the gun to his other hand. "Turn around and open the trunk."

"Why?"

"Just fucking do it, black man."

LaDon turned and slipped one hand under the trunk. He waited.

"Open it. I said to open it."

Ginny said, "Eddie, do I have to watch this?"

"Shut the fuck up. Open it, motherfucker."

LaDon tilted his head to one side, shook it. "You sure you want to—"

"Open it, motherfucker! And get your ass inside!"

LaDon opened the trunk. There it was: the pump-action Savage. Loaded, too. He reached down and grabbed the gun. While he did it, he heard Eddie's voice saying something about how he should stop, that he was going to get his ass shot. But LaDon didn't care—Eddie's plan was to shoot him and put him in the trunk, take his body somewhere else. This was never the grave. It was the murder scene. As LaDon spun, he raised the Savage and leveled it at Eddie.

Eddie shrank backwards, stumbled, caught himself. He still had the gun aimed at LaDon, but his hand shook. And shook. And shook.

LaDon moved forward—he pumped the Savage, put a cartridge in the chamber.

"What are you doing? No, man. I was just fucking with you."

"Go on and shoot my ass," LaDon said. He watched Ginny sprint into the trees. She looked like a shadow slipping off into a fantasy forest. Her hair spread out behind her as she moved. "Squeeze the trigger. You say you want to, go ahead."

Eddie stopped moving. He steeled himself for a moment, steadied his hand. His mouth screwed up below his nose, like a hole closing in on itself.

LaDon shot him, pumped the shotgun again. The blast rang in LaDon's head for a minute. When it cleared, he heard Eddie's moans.

Eddie swooned to the ground as the pain ran through him, like a man falling to his knees for prayer. He dropped the gun and put his hands in his lap. Through his moans, he said, "You shot me in the dick. You god-damn motherfucker. You shot me in the dick."

LaDon kicked the gun away from Eddie. He looked

at the black liquid between Eddie's fingers, felt vomit gurgling in his stomach. He forced it back down and said, "It's hard to be a pimp. Real hard when you don't have no junk."

"You going to take me to a hospital?" Eddie collapsed onto his side. He curled into a ball.

LaDon tilted his head to look Eddie in the eyes. He squinted at the dickless pimp and said, "No, sir. I don't think I will." LaDon lifted the Savage and shot Eddie in the chest. He nodded and stood up straight, pumped the Savage again. He thought better of that and walked over to the Cutlass, stashed the shotgun in the front. He closed the trunk and walked back to Eddie's body. La-Don found the keys to his Cutlass in Eddie's front pocket. He tossed them up and down in his right hand and watched the trees. After a minute or two, LaDon walked into the orchard—might as well find Ginny and give her ass a ride back into the city.

FORTY-THREE

Echo started at the bar where he met Glanson. That dingy place where they drank before Echo shot the old man. Too bad about that. For the old man, at least. Using the bar as a center point, he cruised the streets in a grid, north to south, west to east. But he didn't see any signs for marijuana dispensaries. What he decided to do, after rolling in the Elantra for three hours, was get out and walk the main avenue. It ran for blocks and blocks, endless rows of fruterias, liquor stores, Pentecostal churches, and your occasional restaurant or shoe repair shop. He felt a little like he was in a foreign country, how it was to be in a small town in Eye-Rack and think, shit, these people live a lot like I do.

After a few blocks, Echo spotted a corner market with a young guy sitting behind the counter. He walked in and waved. The kid—nineteen, maybe?—was reading a low rider magazine, but he raised his eyes and studied Echo with defensive curiosity. A dangerous job, manning the counter at a corner market. Especially on the late night or early morning shift. Echo walked to the bank of coolers along the far wall, decided to buy a tallboy of Pabst, sip on it while he walked.

At the counter, the kid rang up the beer. "Three

dollars, plus the tax."

Echo counted out bills from his wallet, placed four on the counter. As the kid made change, Echo said, "You know where I can get a little weed, man? I'm not talking on the street. I'm talking the legit way, one of these shops they got."

The kid handed over the change and raised his eyebrows. His face was thick featured, almost puffed up, like a drunk. "Why you asking me?"

"Why? I'm new in the neighborhood." Echo smiled. "I just want to get high, my friend."

The kid looked over Echo's shoulder, brought his gaze back to Echo's smile. "You go two blocks down, take a right. There's a place next to the auto shop. It doesn't have a sign. You find it because of the tinted windows. There's metal bars behind them. You have to peek inside."

"Nice, brother. Thanks for the intel."

The kid nodded.

Echo said, "Don't worry, I won't tell Mommy and Daddy."

He stood in the shadows across the street, beneath an awning outside an abandoned sandwich shop. He drank his tallboy and licked his lips. The dispensary was right next to an auto shop, discreet with its tinted windows and unlabeled front door. He doubted it was licensed. More likely that the big black man and Glanson's lady tried to ply their trade under the radar.

That interested Echo because it meant Glanson's pal, the guy with the armored van service, was taking money from everybody—not just licensed dispensaries. It meant he cornered the marijuana money and, unless there were other services, he had a shit ton of money locked up in that storage facility down south. Echo decided to wait it out, see if the black dude showed his face. It was almost eight in the morning and there was a desayunos place around the corner. He might get himself some huevos rancheros and come on back. But for now, he'd wait.

Sitting in the dark shadows and sipping his beer reminded Echo of Eye-Rack. All the shit he'd done, all the suck he'd embraced. He remembered waiting outside some prince whoever-the-fuck's palace while an explosives team cleared the place. Him and Glanson with another guy, a crazy fucker named Rico. They took a position inside an abandoned house. It surprised Echo how bare the place was—he figured the family took their valuables, but the furniture too? Rugs in every room, but little else. The three of them got up on the roof, crouched together and watched the street north and south, listened to the bomb guys talking shit on the radio. It was dark out in the early morning, but hot as fuck.

Echo said, "I'm sick of sweating, man." He pried at the damp fabric around his neck.

Glanson laughed at him. Glanson always laughed at the weirdest shit.

Rico said, "It's getting hot in here."

"Fuck that song." Echo hated it.

"Don't be saying that, homie. That man's from where I come from."

"Fuck, Rico," Glanson said. "Where'd you learn how to talk?"

"Speak," Echo said.

"From the streets, homie. Not like you two country cowboys."

Glanson laughed and said, "You're just like every other mofo I come across. You learned to talk from rap albums. Don't try to act all gangster around me."

"Man, the fuck you know about it?"

"I know you won't do shit—that's what I know."

Rico got to his knees, brought his rifle around to the front of his body.

Echo pulled a switchblade from his boot and flicked it open. He waved it between the two soldiers and grinned. "Don't bring a knife to a gunfight, motherfuckers."

Both men laughed.

Echo said, "We're supposed to be watching this fucking street. Open your eyes."

And that's what they did, watched the street for three hours. Telling dirty jokes now and again. Trying to make like they'd been fucked harder than the next guy. And by prettier girls. Three fucking kids sitting around waiting for something to shoot at. Later, after the bomb guys finished, the whole squad wandered around the palace. They found a room full of fucking gold, solid gold bricks just stacked on the carpet like fucking... Echo didn't know like what. And all this fancy art hung from the walls, shit that didn't mean much to Echo. But the captain had him some college, and he kept going on and on about cultural legacy and the myriad artistic achievements of Islam. To Echo, it was another rich guy's house. He lied to himself and said it didn't matter.

But it did.

The gold mattered to him. Not so much the art, but the gold.

He finished his Pabst and leaned back against the wall, deep in the shadows. The streets were coming alive with traffic and delivery trucks. He heard the brushing sound of a city bus passing on the avenue and a couple middle school boys wandered past him while they talked shit about professional basketball. For a second, just for a second, Echo closed his eyes.

FORTY-FOUR

"You can drop me back on the boulevard—right where you picked me up." Ginny ran her hands over her thighs. She had the jitters and LaDon could see it. A second later, as he steered onto the freeway and hit seventy-five, she said, "Wait a minute. Take me to the Greyhound station. The one downtown. And I need fifty bucks. Can you do that?"

LaDon kept his eyes on the road. The pump-action Savage was on the floorboard, beneath his knees. He had the .45 he took from Eddie there too. The way things were going in his life, LaDon wanted some guns where he could reach them. He moved them into the fast lane, decided on what to say to Ginny. He settled on, "That man of yours, he was a real piece of work. I bet you really miss him, huh?"

"I guess."

"You guess? A man just lost his life and you—"

"You didn't have to shoot him," she said.

"Is that right?" LaDon felt blood run into his cheeks. His body was jacked on adrenaline, but this girl still got him pissed off. "You saw, he was going to do me—am I wrong?"

"No," she said leaning her head against the window.

"But you still had a choice."

"Christ."

"That's taking the Lord's name in—"

"Fuck the lord," LaDon said. "And fuck you too. I gave you a chance to get out of here, away from your man. And you go right back to him. What for?" The last bit was a question, but LaDon didn't expect an answer. If there was an answer, Ginny didn't have it. Nobody did. Another one of those questions nobody had the answer to, he thought. The whole world running off questions without answers. He shook his head and bit the corner of his mouth.

"I don't know."

LaDon moved the Cutlass up to eighty, scanned the rearview mirror. Scattered headlights faded behind them. "This is what it takes to get free of somebody. I'm taking you down to the bus station. I swear, I don't want to see you in this city again."

"You won't."

They drove in silence until LaDon hit the first exit for downtown. He headed west on Market, made a turn onto a one-way street. They passed the Salvation Army, all the bums huddled in blankets out front. Two dirty guys in ponchos warmed their hands by a trash can fire.

Ginny rubbed her eyes and yawned. "I can't believe we just left him there, out in the open."

"It ain't me that's going to bury him."

On Imperial he weaved between city buses and de-livery trucks, rolled to the curb outside the bus station. The street was empty of foot traffic and the city was quiet except for engine noise. He looked at Ginny as she gathered her slumped body.

"You know," he said, "I didn't never want to kill—"

"It doesn't matter," she said while rummaging through her purse. She stopped and leaned back in the seat. "I lost my virginity at fourteen. Can you believe that?"

"Look, Ginny, I'm not the guy to—"

"You want to help me, right? Isn't that why you fucked Eddie up, and why you shot him tonight? Looking at it now, sitting here, I'm thinking you want to help me."

LaDon thought: finally, she gets it.

"And if you want to help me, just listen to me talk for five fucking seconds."

He kept his mouth shut.

She said, "Fourteen years old. I was into softball and makeup and emo bands. That was me—who I was. You know, it's not that I didn't know anything about sex. It's that I didn't know anything about love. Because my dad, he…That doesn't matter either. The point is, I lost it at fourteen and after that I started running around with older guys, some crazy girls. Because, you know, I lost who I was. I lost more than what the body is—it was a thing inside me. My heart. My head. And next thing I know, I'm walking around in a city I don't know, and there's this guy—Eddie—and he always knows what to say when I feel lost. Like, he gave me a direction, pointed me where I needed to go. He's dead and, I guess, I'm ashamed. No, I don't guess. I am ashamed. How pitiful am I? I did what this guy said for, Jesus, eighteen months. Horrible things. Stuff I wouldn't make up to put in a story." She sniffed a bit, ran a finger along her cheek.

LaDon said, "Only person needs to be ashamed is Eddie. Plus all those guys who did what they did to you. Because it's them who—"

"Women too," Ginny said.

"Huh?"

"Some women fucked me too. You'd be surprised."

"Okay, look. Why don't you stop—"

Ginny placed a hand on LaDon's thigh, patted it. "Stop worrying about me. I just wanted to put it out there, so you can understand me a little bit. After what you did, I wanted you to know."

LaDon nodded while he studied Ginny's profile. He wanted to remember the sharp, delicate lines of her face. The upturned nose. The high cheekbones. That brush of dark hair over her ears. He took his wallet from his pocket and pulled out all the money he had—three-four hundred. Around there. He handed the money to Ginny.

She took it. After, she opened the door and got out, bent to look in at him. "Thanks for this. I don't plan on seeing you ever again. That okay with you?"

He nodded again.

She slammed the door.

LaDon waited until he saw Ginny enter the bus station. Once she was inside, he pulled away from the curb, looked for a place to make a U-turn—he needed to get back on the freeway.

Back at the dispensary, LaDon searched through Jessie's paperwork and computer files. He didn't want anything traced back to him. He erased the computer hard drive, removed it with a screwdriver, and banged it against the cement floor. When it was good and cracked, he tossed it in the garbage. Most of the paperwork was spreadsheets, names of weed strains and daily sales numbers. God, they did okay together in this business. No, a hell of a lot better than okay. Too bad it needed to end. Or that it ended when Jessie stopped breathing. LaDon took a seat in Jessie's office chair, leaned back and put his feet on the desk next to the Savage. He put his hands behind his head and savored the musty smell of marijuana and money.

The safe behind him was empty, and he already packed the remaining weed into plastic containers. LaDon had no idea what to do with all that—maybe give it to Zim over at The Zip Zap Bar, see if the man could get them something for it.

Last thing to do was wait for the security man and let him know the deal. Sorry, pal. Me and Jessie are out of business. Me, for a little while. Her? Forever. And then some.

About two hours later, while he sipped cheap coffee with powder creamer, LaDon saw the security man's van pull up on the closed-circuit television screen. He got out, one hand on his 9mm, looked both ways, and punched the outside buzzer. LaDon unlocked the door, watched on the other television screen as Abel entered the waiting room, smiled at the camera above the door. LaDon stood and walked past the two glass cases now empty of weed and edibles, opened the door.

Abel sauntered in, thought he was all hot shit. "Hey, buddy. I'm here to pick up the moola."

LaDon walked back through the display cases, took his seat behind Jessie's desk.

"Oh, wow," Abel said. "You the big man now?" His right hand rested on that nine.

Abel's eyes touched on the Savage, lingered on it.

"It's a cheap piece, this shottie," said LaDon. "But it'll do the trick. In a pinch, you know?"

"You don't have to tell me. I got a buddy torn to pieces by an IED made from a Folgers coffee can and a handful of rusty bolts."

"Fuck me."

"Yeah, you can say that again. Fuck it all, matter of fact."

"I wanted to let you know," LaDon said, "that we're going out of business."

"Shit."

"Going to have to sever our contract."

Abel moved back toward the door and touched the handle. "I'm sorry to hear that. By my count, you were doing okay..." He hesitated before saying, "What happened to your partner, the looker?"

"Dead," LaDon said without emotion. "Like your partner."

They stared at each other. LaDon rested one hand on the Savage while Abel kept a hand on the 9mm.

The room seemed empty somehow, though two men with guns stared bullets at each other.

Abel finally said, "Strange couple of deaths."

LaDon nodded. He wondered about the security man then, saw how the man took in everything about the room: The three security cameras pointing down at them, the empty glass display cases, the cracked hard drive in the waste basket, all the shredded documents in plastic trash bags. Like Abel was casing the office, making sense of everything and putting it all together.

Shit, LaDon thought, if I want that money—for real— I may have to kill this motherfucker. Either that, or he'll put it together who robbed his ass.

He'll put it together fast. And he'll come after me.

Abel brushed the nine with his index finger. "Did you

kill my buddy?"

"Christ, no. Didn't know the man besides when he came in here."

"But the girl, you didn't want—"

"I was friends with Jessie. And, yeah, we were part-ners. But there wasn't anything else there."

"I guess, the way it looks for both of them to be dead in a couple days, seems to me that—"

"Because I'm sitting here and breathing," LaDon said, "it don't make me a killer."

"No," Abel said. "You might just be the lucky one."

"Me and you both."

Abel opened the door, backed into the waiting room. "Seems our business together is over."

LaDon lifted the Savage and held it across his chest. "All finished," he said. "But I need that money, what you've been holding for us."

"Why don't I by bring by tomorrow? Same time, okay?"

"You do that. I'd appreciate it."

Abel closed the door and LaDon watched on the closed-circuit as he hurried through the waiting room, exited the dispensary, and hopped into his white Econo-line. The van pulled away from the curb, left the televi-sion with a static view of the exterior sidewalk and part of the street. The closed-circuit wasn't too clear, but LaDon thought he read the expression on Abel's face as he drove away. No doubt in LaDon's mind...the man was scared.

FORTY-FIVE

Echo cursed himself when he saw the white Econoline van pull up outside the unmarked dispensary. You dumb fuck, he thought, you don't have a fucking ride. Right, he walked here after leaving the Elantra on one of the nearby neighborhood streets. What, a quarter or half mile from here? Glanson's boss, the other war vet named Abel, climbed out of the van and entered the dispensary. What am I going to do? Can't just stand here, you dumb fuck. At some point, you need to follow somebody. The big black guy, probably. Alright. Fuck.

Echo walked fast to the corner, turned onto the avenue and started jogging.

The street looked different in the late morning. More foot traffic and cars honking at pedestrians. He noticed a few police squad cars as they zoomed past him. Fuck it. Echo was white in a Latino neighborhood—be like winning the lottery if the cops stopped him. He jogged past the liquor store and noticed an older guy behind the counter, spitting image of the kid from last night. A family affair, hawking sugar and tobacco to the masses. Alright, what street did he park on...Thirty-seventh? Or maybe it was Cherokee? No, Echo remembered the numbered street name. He turned down the street, still jogging, and clicked the key fob a few times. It took a block and a half, but the Elantra's horn honked twice and Echo hustled over, got into the car.

He made a hurried right turn onto the avenue and had Tupac on the CD player before he pulled to the curb outside the dispensary—right behind the white van, matter of fact. And, sure as shit, Abel came out and hopped into the van, took off down the street. One thing Echo noticed: Abel didn't have a bag of money with him. And why in the fuck was that?

The black dude, Echo told himself, he's going to take it. All that money, man.

Too bad he can't take the money with him into the afterlife. That was for goddamn certain.

Echo went through the entire Tupac catalog while he waited for the black dude.

It surprised him that his waitress fling liked hip-hop so much. He remembered a guy in the service, black guy with lots of tattoos, saying mainstream hip-hop was more for white people than black people. Echo laughed at that, but now he wondered. The fuck did Tupac have to say to some skinny white girl living near the beach? Not that Tupac didn't have shit to say—he did. To Echo, it was just that…He caught himself and grinned: here you are listening to every song the man ever made. Talking shit about a white girl who likes a beat and some flow.

The black dude walked out—with two large duffel bags—around two in the afternoon, during the chorus for "Hit 'Em Up." Echo thought that fit the scene.

Like a goddamn sheepskin rubber.

* * *

He followed the gold Cutlass down University to the 805, got on the freeway behind it. Saw the big black guy's left elbow hanging out the window. This motherfucker rode around cool as fuck after seeing his partner get killed. Another surprise to Echo. But it told him something: This dude had a history, and it included violence. Death, too. That had to be the case for this guy to cruise through town like he was out on a Sunday drive after seeing a friend get shot.

Echo still didn't know whether the woman made it, but he doubted it. Otherwise, he imagined the black guy might be at the hospital, waiting around for some doctor to give him the good news.

Nope. So, what now?

The Cutlass exited after a couple miles and swung east onto a surface street. Echo followed a few car lengths behind, certain the black guy didn't know he was being followed. The Cutlass swung left again onto a residential street, pulled into the drive near a small apartment building. Red trim and white stucco, kind of a mission-style place with graffiti on the sidewalk. Echo drove right past, didn't even look over at the guy. He parked in the first open space he found and watched in the rearview as the black guy entered a lower level apartment. By now Echo was through with the official Tupac catalog. He found an old Ice Cube CD and threw that into the player. Turned it down so most of what he heard was the bass thump.

About two hours later, here came the black dude with another duffel. This one in black and a lot bigger. Clothes, Echo thought. A bunch of clothes and maybe some other personal shit thrown in with them. He had two other small cases with him—they looked to Echo like tiny bazookas. Some kind of weapons the guy wanted with him? No, something else. And then Echo had it. They were fly rods, for fly fishing. The black dude threw everything into the trunk, double checked his billfold, and pulled out another small item—a fucking passport.

Echo grinned when he saw that. He thought, where the fuck are you going, big man?

Down south, that's where.

Echo knew the way. They rolled along the same streets and into the same industrial area where Echo followed the security man a few days prior. How about this? Was the black dude going to collect his money, take it with him to wherever the fuck he was going fly fishing? The Cutlass stayed under the speed limit and, once he knew where they were headed, Echo hung back a quarter mile. He didn't want to get caught trailing the man. In a case like this, Echo knew that surprising the black man was necessary. Like in the apartment. Except this time Echo needed to cap his ass, put some lead into the man. Make him bleed.

The Cutlass made the final turn and Echo slowed when he reached the corner, nosed the Elantra forward until he saw the Cutlass slide alongside a warehouse. The red taillights shut down and the black dude's arm dangled out the window. He was going to wait. Echo made the turn, crossed over the centerline, and parked the Elantra behind a line of trash dumpsters. He could see the Cutlass through the space between them. Echo rolled down the windows and turned Ice Cube up a wee bit. It was a nice evening already, the sun ducking behind the metal buildings and leaving pink light high up against flat irregular clouds. He liked the feel of the air in the evenings, made him look forward to a few drinks and a burger. But first Echo needed to get this money.

Looked like he needed to bury two motherfuckers to do it. Echo leaned forward in the driver's seat, removed the black .45 he kept lodged against his back. He set the gun in his lap and leaned back against the headrest. He thought: Wait until the black man makes his move, get the two of these motherfuckers together at once. And then what? End it—that's what.

FORTY-SIX

LaDon parked and unlatched his seatbelt. He used the side view mirror to watch the dark Elantra—trailing him all the way from the city—slide around the corner and disappear behind a line of trash dumpsters. The car had tinted windows and LaDon couldn't identify the driver, but he bet the tip of his dick it was the same dude who shot Jessie. And who took a shot at him. LaDon hung his hand out the window and tapped a slow beat on the door panel. He still had the Savage close at hand, right there on the floorboard. He also had the .45 he took from Eddie. It was sitting on the passenger seat now, where he could get to it.

He watched the mirror and imagined how the night might unravel.

The money: he doubted Abel would bring it to him. The problem was that two people were dead. Dead people make living people scared. And Abel, LaDon knew, sensed something was wrong. That his employee, maybe, got put down by one of his customers. Read: LaDon Marcus Garvey Charles. Still, LaDon entertained talking like an adult to the man, getting him to see the truth. Why would I kill anybody? I'm doing good. Me and Jessie have something. Why am I going to fuck that up by killing some dude? No reason for it. But LaDon knew Abel wouldn't see that. Instead, he'd see himself as next in line, a dead man walking.

Alright. Let's play it out like this: I see Abel pull up, enter the storage facility. I go into the office and talk to the clerk, wave the Savage in his face until he opens up. Make sure he knows I'll tear him to spaghetti if he calls the cops.

LaDon squinted into the dusk light, tried to see who was inside the storage facility office. Looked like one person sitting behind the desk, but he couldn't be sure. Might be somebody in a back office, too. A middle management hero.

Fine, there's two then. Maybe I make them come with me. We cruise through the hallways until we find Abel unloading all his money. All those gray duffel bags filled with cash. I pump the Savage and tell him what the deal is: give me three or four bags and that's it. All I want. My share from the past month or so.

What, you think Abel's going to hand it to you? Just like that?

What he's going to ask is, "What the fuck happened to Jessie and Glanson?" Shit, he's got to ask that. No other choice left to the man. It doesn't happen like that, LaDon. You don't get to escape the killing. You already did one last night, and now you got to do another one. His eyes left the boxy gray buildings of the storage facility and moved back to the mirror. One, yeah. And maybe you got to do two. LaDon reached between his legs and picked up the Savage. Light for a shotgun. Easy to hold and carry. Made you feel like it didn't have killing power.

But LaDon knew it did. Yeah, bet your sweet ass it did.

* * *

The street was empty except for LaDon in the Cutlass, the dark Elantra behind the dumpsters, and a shitty GMC Jimmy truck parked outside the storage facility. The warehouses seemed empty, not in use, and the street dead-ended about forty yards past the storage place—the only exit was to the main road. It was near dark, the pink dusk having toned down to a soft blue already going black. LaDon heard the van's brakes squealing before he saw it. A second later, the white Econoline turned onto the street and LaDon watched it approach in the side view mirror. The white van pulled alongside the Cutlass but didn't slow. No way that Abel knew LaDon's car. No reason for him to know it. LaDon leaned as far back in his seat as possible, watched the white van pull into the parking lot with its squealing brakes.

Abel rolled down the driver's side window and punched a code into the gate box. The metal gate creaked and clanged as it rolled open—the white van pulled through and vanished into the maze of gray buildings. The gate closed.

LaDon took the .45 from the passenger seat and slipped it into his coat. He wore black leather tonight, a jacket that ran too tight for him to zip up but which he liked for style points. He already had the Savage in his lap. He opened the door and stepped onto the street, let the door shut with a soft click. He looked back at the line of dumpsters. LaDon knew the shooter planned to follow.

Alright, LaDon, it's time. Now or fucking never.

He jogged across the street, the shotgun hidden along his leg. Not too noticeable in the near dark.

He crossed the parking lot and looked for the white van through the gate. Didn't see it. He kept moving across the lot until he reached the office. He placed a hand on the door and turned to watch the street. LaDon didn't see the shooter, but he did hear a clear and discernible sound:

Far off down the street, a car door slammed.

FORTY-SEVEN

A sing-song tone announced LaDon's entry to the office.

The guy behind the desk leaned forward to see who was coming in so late and his ponytail fell over his shoulder. He brushed it back with a tattooed hand and said, "What can I do for you?"

LaDon didn't try to hide the Savage. The office smelled of weed and he made a show of sniffing the air. Like a priest in a rose garden. "I'm here to meet a friend."

Ponytail stepped out from behind the desk. His eyes were red and circled by dark patches of skin.

LaDon said, "I know how this looks but I promise not to make a mess."

Ponytail scratched his cheek and nodded. "I mean, yeah—it's better if you don't make a mess."

"Thing is," LaDon said, "I'm going to have to, you know, tie you up."

"Ah, c'mon, man. That's not cool."

LaDon lifted the Savage and shook it, like what you'd do with an empty glass at a bar.

"Okay, I get it." Ponytail pointed at LaDon, something occurring to him in the moment. "Are you here for that pot guy too?"

"Too? You saying there's—"

"Another guy, yeah. He followed me one day and gave me three hundred bucks. Said to keep him in the loop about the money, let him in when he shows up."

"White dude?"

"Yeah, wait…" Ponytail squinted at LaDon, or past him. "That's the guy right there."

The sing-song chant sounded and LaDon turned to see the guy who killed Jessie less than twenty-four hours ago—same motherfucker who tried to shoot LaDon. He carried a bulky-looking .45 in his right hand. He smiled. No, grinned. Wide, too.

He said, "Howdy."

LaDon took a step backwards to where he had pony-tail and the killer in sight, like he was a boxing judge. He kept the Savage at his side, used his empty hand to pat the .45 through his leather jacket. He sniffed that weed aroma again and curled his upper lip.

Ponytail shook his head and said, "Holy fuck."

The killer said to LaDon, "We haven't met yet. My pals call me Echo."

"LaDon. LaDon Charles." He bit the inside of his bottom lip and waited for Echo to say more. It didn't happen so LaDon added, "I was just going to tie up our man here and put him in a closet."

"Fuck me," ponytail said.

"I believe our man goes by Elvis."

LaDon looked at ponytail, who nodded.

"Elvis it is," Elvis said. "You mind if I take another hit before, you know?" He licked his lips and rubbed his hands together.

LaDon said, "Go right ahead, hound dog."

* * *

Elvis told them Abel rented three storage units in building four.

LaDon and Echo walked together down the center lane that bisected the storage facility with all its corrugated steel doors closed like eyelids and the night coming down hard on them. There were yellowish lights all along the lane, but a few were out and LaDon got jumpy walking through the dark spaces with Echo at his side.

They didn't say anything to each other after tying Elvis up and putting him in a closet. Was there anything to say? Here they were, two guys wanting the same money. And not sure how they were going to handle each other.

The storage facility was comprised of four buildings situated across from each other, all intersected by two criss-crossed lanes wide enough for moving trucks. LaDon didn't see any cars or trucks until they made a right down the intersecting lane. At the end of the pavement, parked next to the high chain-link fence, was the white Econoline van. The two back doors were wide open but the van was empty. Stripped of its rear seats. Next to the van, the storage building's door was propped open with a large rock.

LaDon tightened his grip on the Savage, brought it up so it crossed his waist, ready to swing up and fire. He hugged the building as he walked. Echo moved to the opposite side of the lane, across from LaDon, and kept his .45 trained on the open door.

They heard whistling from inside the building. It floated out on the night air, cut the odd silence of abandoned industrial buildings. LaDon couldn't catch the tune, but it had a nice tone and melody. Why not whistle while you work?

As they moved toward the door, the whistling got louder.

Echo stopped when he was almost—but not quite—directly across from the open door.

LaDon lifted the Savage and tried to stay a few feet behind Echo, though he was closest to the door on his side of the lane. He didn't want to give Echo an easy shot at him.

The whistling stopped.

Abel's voice came from the building corridor: "Who the fuck are you?"

"I used to pal around with Glanson," Echo said. "When we were in the shit."

Abel still hadn't seen LaDon because he stopped short of the doorway and crouched with the Savage. He kept one eye on Echo who had the .45 aimed straight into the open doorway.

Abel said, "You the one fried his ass?"

"He was already dead."

LaDon shook his head and breathed heavy.

Echo said, "Don't, motherfucker."

A bright flash erupted from the doorway. It was followed by the sharp sound of pistol fire. After that, LaDon heard only footsteps. He squinted to account for the sudden flash's effect on his vision and, when he adjusted again to the dark, he saw Echo slumped against the storage building. His gun was on the ground and both hands were clutched against his stomach.

"Looks like you lose," LaDon said.

"He shot me."

"It goes that way sometimes."

"Fuck you, man."

LaDon crept forward, peeked into the doorway. It was dark again in the corridor. LaDon moved into the doorway and motion sensor lights popped on, made him squint to see. It made sense now why he saw the flash before hearing the gunfire. As he moved down the corridor past the corrugated steel doors with their beefy U-locks, the lights popped on slightly ahead of him. Reflected against the pure white ceiling and walls, the light amplified in brightness along the replicated rows of steel doors. After twenty feet or so, LaDon stopped—he imagined Abel around the next corner, waiting for those lights to pop on so he could shoot holes in the first silhouette he saw. LaDon chanced a look back outside. Echo was slumped in darkness. He didn't appear to be moving. Okay, LaDon told himself, let's think about this for one minute.

He hesitated while he thought what to do. The Savage felt heavier then, like it was made of lead.

The motion sensor lights clicked off and he was in darkness.

The storage building emitted the regular sounds: The soft buzz of electricity. An air conditioning unit humming somewhere. The irregular chirp of crickets from outside. He sniffed the building's artificial air.

Listened for footsteps, breathing, cracking joints.

Nothing.

Wait, he told himself. Wait for it.

A minute passed—no motion sensor lights popping on and no new noise.

And then he heard the nearly imperceptible clink of a U-lock closing.

LaDon pumped the Savage, sprinted down the corridor with the lights popping on ahead of him, as if he was running into a tunnel of light. He reached another corridor and turned right, saw another tunnel of light unfurling at the end of the hall. He fired the Savage, felt it kick hard against his collarbone. He grunted. Pumped and fired again. He moved forward with the shotgun pointed out ahead of him, into the brightly lit corridor.

He didn't see Abel, but he heard him.

Like air blowing through shredded canvas.

LaDon crouched and turned the corner at the next corridor. There wasn't much blood. What little there was clung to Abel's shirt, shown through like a faded stain.

Abel groaned.

LaDon moved forward in the bright lights, kneeled beside the dying man and patted down his pockets. He pulled out a set of keys. "You going to tell me what number?"

"Fuck yourself." Blood ran over Abel's lips, trickled onto his clean-shaven chin.

Both men were still and the motion sensor lights shut off, put them in the dark.

LaDon cleared his throat and stood—the lights popped on again. Abel kept trying to take air into his mouth, like a stingray flipped onto its back. He moaned once more.

LaDon shook his head.

He turned back to the other corridor and began trying the keys in each lock. On his fifth try, a silver U-lock popped open. LaDon lifted the corrugated steel door. Inside, he counted twenty-seven duffel bags—some black and some gray—piled atop each other. He whistled the same tune he heard Abel whistling. How many could he carry out of there? Four? Five?

Another of Abel's moans floated through the building.

LaDon sniffed the artificial air again and unzipped one of the duffel bags. Like he thought, packs of small bills in rubber bands and Ziploc bags. He shoved the Savage into the bag, left it unzipped. He shrugged into one of the duffels and wore it like a backpack. With his left hand, he carried two bags. In his right, he carried another two, including the open one with the Savage right where he could get at it. He started out of the building, a tunnel of bright lights both illuminating and erasing his path. Goddamn, LaDon told himself, I'm making this shit happen.

LaDon walked with caution toward the storage facility's front gate.

What tripped LaDon up: Echo wasn't lying there dead like he expected. The man was gone. Left a puddle of blood on the cement. Around the corner maybe? Nope, not there either.

So LaDon approached the gate with one eye on his Savage. Only one round left in it. His heart beating like hell up into his throat. Careful, baby. Don't fuck up right at the finish line. He got to the gate and peered through the slats, saw his Cutlass shining gold beneath the soft glow of a yellow streetlight.

Make it quick, LaDon.

He punched the security code and the gate moved. No time to untie Elvis. Oh, well. He'd be alright. LaDon squeezed through the gate and jogged across the parking lot, past the beat-to-hell Jimmy, into the dark street. He got to the Cutlass, felt his heart beat all the way into his forehead. He dropped the bags, grabbed the Savage, and scanned the street. No Echo.

LaDon opened the driver's side door.

The first bullet hit him in the right shoulder, turned him sideways. LaDon caught a glimpse of Echo lying prone in the rear seat. He tried to bring up the Savage with his right hand, squeezed off a shot that missed wildly, sprayed gut shot through his fucking windshield. The glass spider-webbed like thin ice. A second shot plugged him in the right hip, a bullet that ripped through the driver's seat. LaDon staggered back a step, saw Echo rest the .45 in his lap, close his bright eyes.

So dark back there, I didn't see him. Fuck me. Fuck me. Fuck me.

He saw a smear of red on the front seat's headrest. A bloody fingerprint on the steering wheel. LaDon tried to bring the Savage up again, but he didn't have the strength.

Bringing out the .45 somehow seemed pointless.

He dropped the shotgun and went to his knees, collapsed to all fours.

The pain ran through him like a hundred sledge-hammers pounding his bones. Then a funny thing happened—LaDon went numb. He fell on his right side and flipped onto his back. He stared up at the night sky. He didn't see one damn star with the low cloud cover. No, it was just gray-black with a big hazy moon trying to come through. But failing. He didn't hear Echo move and some part of LaDon knew they were both going to die here, on a dumpy street in a rundown warehouse district. You get greedy, and shit goes bad. LaDon knew that, but he got greedy anyway.

LaDon heard the slow revving of an engine down the

street. The crackle of tires rolling across pavement. The familiar body shape of an eighty-three hatchback Corolla. Two mismatched hubcaps rolled past him. Headlights swung clockwise and hit the gold Cutlass. Stayed there. A door opened.

Footsteps.

A silhouette appeared above LaDon, bent down to look at him. "Goddamn, LaDon. It don't look like neither of you all is gonna make it. It's a shit show out here."

"Moonie?"

"Yeah, brother."

"I was supposed to call you…"

"Call never came," Moonie said. "Figured I'd come on down here and take a look myself."

"I got popped."

"That's a fact," Moonie said. "Shot out your windshield too, brother-man."

"Fuck my windshield."

"Yes, sir."

LaDon said, "The bags are full of money."

Moonie cleared his throat and unzipped the closest duffel bag. When he saw what was inside, he whistled. He zipped the bag closed, squinted at LaDon. "You want me to hold it for you?"

"You the one," LaDon said. He counted them off in his head: Glanson, Jessie, Echo. And now me. Everybody dead. That leaves only one.

"Come again?"

"The one," LaDon Marcus Garvey Charles said. "You the one."

ACKNOWLEDGMENTS

I always thank my wife for her patience, hard work, and love. I'll add one more thing: Thank you for being such a wonderful mother. I'll thank Charlie, my little son, for his constant joy and humor. Love you, man! I have to thank my best pal Jeremy for his constant support and insight (you know what I mean, brother). Thanks to all the editors I've worked with including Chris Rhatigan and Chris Black. Thanks for choosing this book, Rhatigan—love the work you're doing with all of us crooks and writers. Thanks to the crew at Down & Out, especially Eric Campbell and Lance Wright. You guys put in work. Thanks for doing it. Means the world to all of us writers (and crooks). Thanks to the California electorate—we finally got it right! Much love to my fellow San Diegans. Oh, yeah, and big thanks to stoners everywhere...

Matt Phillips lives in San Diego. His books include *Accidental Outlaws*, *Three Kinds of Fool*, *The Bad Kind of Lucky*, and *Know Me from Smoke*. He has published crime stories across the web at *Yellow Mama*, *Shotgun Honey*, *Near to the Knuckle*, *Out of the Gutter's Flash Fiction Offensive*, *Pulp Metal Magazine*, *Tough Crime*, *Manslaughter Review*, and elsewhere.

MattPhillipsWriter.com

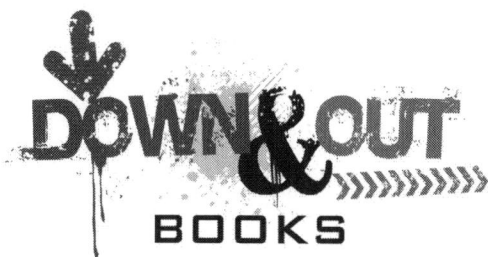

DOWN & OUT BOOKS

On the following pages are a few
more great titles from the
Down & Out Books publishing family.

For a complete list of books and to
sign up for our newsletter,
go to DownAndOutBooks.com.

ALL DUE RESPECT

SHOTGUN HONEY

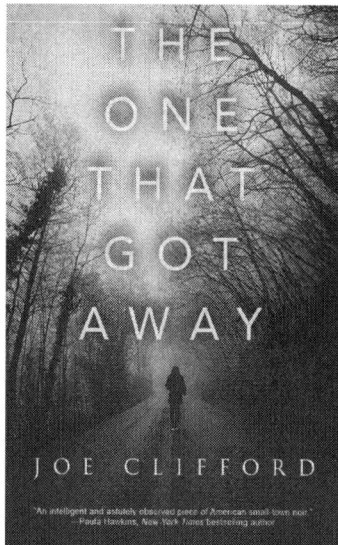

The One That Got Away
Joe Clifford

Down & Out Books
978-1-948235-42-6

In the early 2000s, a string of abductions rocked the small upstate town of Reine, New York. Only one girl survived: Alex Salerno. The killer was sent away. Life returned to normal. No more girls would have to die.

Until another one did…

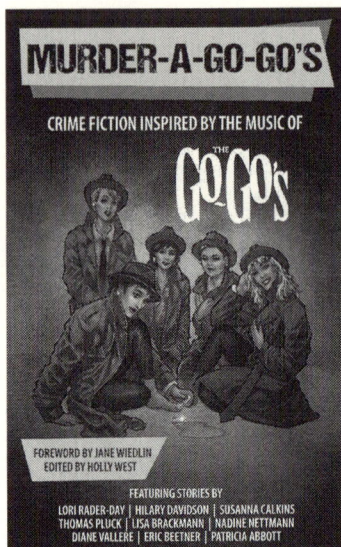

Murder-A-Go-Go's
Crime Fiction Inspired by the Music of The Go-Go's
Edited by Holly West

Down & Out Books
978-1-948235-62-4

The Go-Go's made music on their own terms and gave voice to a generation caught between the bra-burning irreverence of the seventies and the me-first decadence of the eighties.

With a foreword by Go-Go's co-founder Jane Wiedlin and original stories by twenty-five kick-ass authors, editor Holly West has put together an all-star crime fiction anthology.

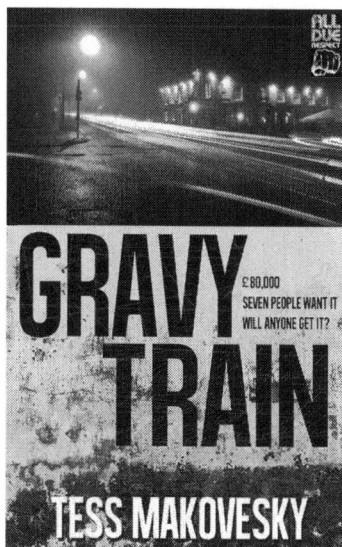

Gravy Train
Tess Makovesky

All Due Respect, an imprint of
Down & Out Books
978-1-64396-006-7

When barmaid Sandra wins eighty grand on a betting scam she thinks she's got it made. But she's reckoned without an assortment of losers and criminals, including a mugger, a car thief and even her own step-uncle George.

As they hurtle towards a frantic showdown by the local canal, will Sandra see her ill-gotten gains again? Or will her precious gravy train come shuddering to a halt?

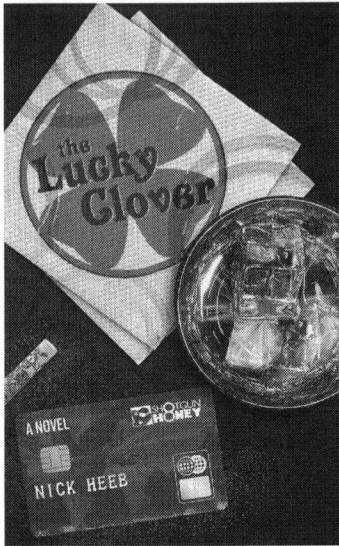

The Lucky Clover
Nick Heeb

Shotgun Honey, an imprint of
Down & Out Books
978-1-948235-69-3

When the Narrator returns to his old haunt, The Lucky Clover, he is looking to forget and recover from his past life's miseries and humiliations by drinking with good friends.

He soon discovers the people closest to him had no interest in his honest intentions, and that violence is the only language spoken in this sparse and hard country he calls home.

Made in the USA
Middletown, DE
09 November 2019